THE WIZARDS OF MAGNOLIA

FUN UNLIMITED

AKSHARA SIVARAJ

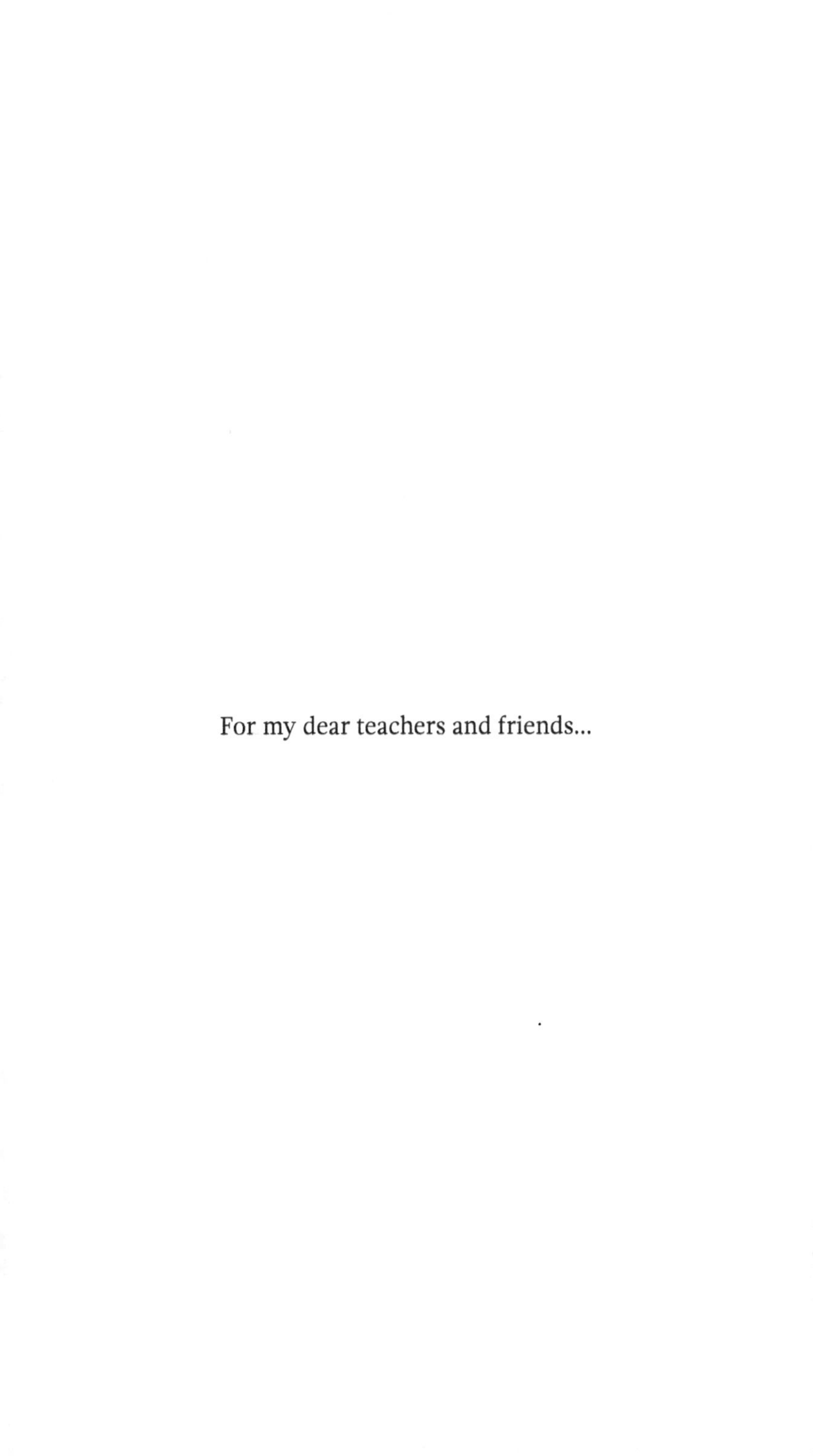

For my dear teachers and friends...

Contents

Contents

Prologue

Have you ever been in a class that has been in so much trouble that you would be scolded at and get complaints from every teacher every single day? Have you ever been in a class whose students support one another, whatever the case may be? Have you ever been in a class that has won the '*Best Class of the Year*' award despite being the most boisterous and troublesome? Well, I sure have!

This book is about all the little quirks and mischiefs one can find in a classroom. Where students fight with one another, throwing books & stationery across the class but are later found laughing together. Where students blast music in the classroom while some stand guard at the door to warn the others to turn down the music when a teacher walks by. Where an entire class covers up for a mishap caused by one/some of their fellow peers, not tattling to the teachers even when enquired.

This story is of the *unison* between the students of this classroom. This story is of the little fights and quarrels that ensue every day in this classroom. This story is of the *camaraderie* between the students of this classroom. This story is of the *guts* they have to stand up for their peers. And most importantly, this story is of the *love* that the students of this class share.

FIRST DAY OF SCHOOL

A number of big yellow buses entered the school gates successively, a larger number of students getting down from each. Each student walked with their heads up high, laughing with their friends (whom they were meeting after a long hiatus) and wearing new shiny uniforms and paper-white shoes. They were sure excited for their school year but disappointed at the end of their 'days of pleasure'.

The amphitheatre of the school was filled with boisterous activity of children pouring in and finding themselves a comfortable place to rest their heavy bags filled with books that they hoped to empty into their lockers as soon as they were assigned one. Meanwhile, the teachers strode towards their cafeteria for an early morning cup of coffee to energise themselves before they were given the responsibility of their students.

"May we all settle down, please," said Ms Charlotte into the microphone, standing atop the dais. "Good morning, everyone! We teachers truly hope you had a well-rested and rejuvenating summer!" While all the Elementary Schoolers whizzed in agreement, the Middle & High

Schoolers booed and groaned in dismay – after all, they had to wake up early in the morning and come to school instead of lying in bed until late afternoon and playing video games all day.

"We have a tradition here in this school to care for our newcomers, may it be teachers, students, or staff. Rest assured, we will make you feel at home!" continued Ms Charlotte, who was clad in a black dress – that had little pink flowers printed on them – with matching shoes. Continuing her speech, she spoke of all the rules & regulations of the school and all the traditions that its students and teachers followed. The uniform pattern and the pattern of the assembly days were stated. Once she was done, she said, "Now, before dispersing, kindly rise for the school song. For those who do not know it, you can begin learning it from your diary as soon as your teachers give them to you!"

Following the 'cringy' song (as the students call it), the boisterous spirits left the amphitheatre and entered the corridors of the higher floors where the Middle & High Schoolers settled into their respective classrooms.

However, the most boisterous classroom of all was this one, in room 114, called *Magnolia*. It was the last class down the corridor, after which there was the staircase, an audio-visual room and a basic laboratory for combined sciences.

The class was found, by its students, to be neatly decorated by its homeroom teacher, Ms Lancy. There was a neat banner opposite the door, stating 'Welcome Magnolia!' and across it was a board full of quotes related to fun learning. The tables were placed tracing the periphery of the room which was a rectangle with a wall down the middle of one of its longer sides. The chairs were placed in a neat rectangle with the teacher's chair & table placed right at the front of the class, in the centre, in front of the whiteboard & projector screen.

As the children came pouring in, they found their seats next to their friends, dropping their bags on the floor with a thud. Finally, when everyone was there, Ms Lancy entered the class and took her seat at the teacher's table, pulling the chair in front of it.

"Good morning, everyone. To all those who do not know me, or know me and may have forgotten me, I am Ms Lancy and I shall be your homeroom teacher for the year," she joked. "Before I move on with what I've planned for you this hour, I would like all the students to introduce themselves to everyone and tell us a little something about yourselves so as to help our new students here get to know you better. Following that, I shall assign each of the new students a buddy who will help them around the school until they find themselves comfortable."

By turns, each student introduced themselves, some with really hilarious introductions.

The first girl to speak was a well-built, tall girl, perhaps the tallest in the class, with glasses and hair going no much further down than her neck. She spoke, "Hello. My name is Stacy. Umm...I don't really know what to say, so you can keep me at that." Everyone giggled.

Next spoke a thin boy, a little above 5 feet tall, who had glasses and rabbit-like teeth. He said, "Hello, my name is Jake, and we lived for many years in the US. I love playing video games, so if you have them as well, I need your server names, so I can play with you."

Following Jake spoke a short & stout boy with hair brushing his eyebrows, "Hello. My name is Jamie, and I love playing football. I have a Siberian husky, and my dad's in the army."

Next spoke a boy who was relatively tall, but not as tall as Stacy. He said hastily and in a rather indecipherable American accent, "Hello. My name is Daniel. My family has relocated from the US, and I say: Hail Hitler!" As he lifted his left hand up in accordance to what he said; the crowd burst into a thousand chuckles.

Following him spoke a girl with curly hair who was rather shy and couldn't seem to frame her sentences properly. All she said was, "Hello. My name is Bethany."

Next came a pale boy who spoke with a bold attitude, "Hello. My name is Adam, and I am British. I have a dog that I saved from the streetside, and I love marine life."

The next child to speak was a boy who had oily hair and continually blinked. He said, "Hello, my name is Harry. I love to play cricket, and I was the class representative of my class last year."

Following him was a girl with hair whose texture was somewhere between curly and wavy. Her hair was let down, and she looked rather rebellious with all the pen marks she had made on her hands. She said, "My name is Alice, and I'm Australian. I have a brother who's really annoying, and I love BTS. BTS for life!"

At this, there was an uprise among the students in agreement. "Quiet down, please. Now you go, Hannah," said Ms Lancy.

The short & stout girl with similar but shorter hair than Alice spoke, "My name is Hannah, and I have fish that I take out by their fins, leave to dry, and then put them back in."

Following a brief conversation regarding the questionable continued existence of Hannah's fish, a short boy named Lewis spoke. He said, "Hi friends, welcome back to my YouTube channel! My name is Lewis, and I have a little brother in pre-primary. I love video games, and I can imitate the voice of Voldemort really well." As he demonstrated this, the class burst into an amused applaud.

Next came a girl with short hair and glasses. She said, "Hello! My name is Holly. I love entomology, so if you find any dead insects, especially butterflies, please do bring them to me. I have a whole collection of insect specimens!" At this, Ms Lancy jokingly said, "If I were you, I would have fallen down dizzy looking at all those insects!" The girl then continued speaking, "Also, if anybody wishes to adopt a dog or dogs, please do let me know. I have 3 Indie puppies – well trained – up for adoption." At this, Ms Lancy yet again spoke, "Oh wow, Holly! I would love to, but I already have a dog. I'll let you know if any of my friends or relatives need it though."

Next was a relatively tall boy with short curly hair. He spoke in a deep voice, "Hello, my name is Samuel. I love football and any type of sports, which is why I spend all my time on the field playing during the breaks."

The next boy, Oliver, had braces on his teeth and was almost as tall as (or taller than) Stacy. He said, "My name is Oliver, and I love to bake. I also love singing, and I am currently on my third level in Trinity vocals. I also have a dog whom I love very dearly."

Next up was a relatively shorter boy who wore studs. He said with a cracked voice, "Hello. My name is Ben, and I too love football & sports in general. I have a little sister in Elementary School, and I have a family estate."

Next, a boy named Jacob introduced himself, saying that he loved wildlife. His speech was very brief and feeble but to the point.

Next up was a girl named Margaret. She had wavy hair and glasses with an almost transparent frame. Her nails were neatly cut, and her hair was neatly combed into a pony that had no way to escape onto her face. She was only around 5 feet tall. Although soft, she boldly said in a polite fashion, "My name is Margaret. I am a trained Kathak dancer, and I also love to sing, read and write. My favourite subject is physics, and I take much interest in space science as well. I lived in a country called Kuwait for the first nine years of my life but was born in Mumbai. I would also like to add that 2 of the 3 new students present here live in the same society as me, so do feel free to approach me even outside of school if you require anything."

Next up was a relatively tall girl with brown-framed glasses and straight hair tied in a pony, some of it falling beside her ears as bangs. She shyly spoke with a soft but solid voice, "My name is Amber. I have a cat named Snowy, and I love Dubai. Dubai best." At this, she gave Margaret a little smirk.

One of the last girls to speak was a well-built, tall girl with curly hair and milky skin. She said, "Hello my name is Amy, and I have a dog called Ginger, who's a Labrador. I love dogs, and I lived in Vietnam for 2 years. My mother wants me to grow tall enough to be able to reach the lofts without needing to step on a chair."

Next up was an extremely tall girl who was much taller than Margaret but shorter than Stacy. She was thin and had almost straight hair with bangs falling down her face, in front of her eyes. She spoke softly, "Hello, my name is Sophie. I have an annoying little brother and have lived in the Netherlands for a few years. I love playing basketball. I really want a phone, but my parents would not give me one."

Finally, the last girl, who was also as tall as Sophie, wore shorts and had her healthy black hair in two neatly done

French braids. She said in a voice almost inaudible, "My name is Eleanor. I love reading, and I am from Chennai. I also take interest in current affairs & politics."

Once all the children had introduced themselves, the three new students – Laura, Thomas and Luke – introduced themselves and told the class about their old schools.

Once everyone was well introduced and the 3 students were assigned buddies, Ms Lancy said, "So kids, I am going to make you all do me a little something. I am going to give each one of you a piece of paper onto which you are going to write a letter to your future self. Please make sure to include your aims & goals for the year. It need not necessarily be academic-related. It could even be wanting to make more friends or being able to read a particular number of books. Whatever it is, I will collect them once you're done. However, I will not read them, so you can write *whatever* you wish to as it is to your own future self. On the last day of school, when you all are a year older, I will return these letters to you. You can then read them and check to see if you have accomplished all that you wanted to. Cool?"

The next ten minutes, the children spent in writing their letters. Finally, when the last of them submitted their letters, Ms Lancy called up a few students to distribute notebooks for each subject to everyone. Many of them wrote their sections from the previous academic year! Realising too late what they had done, they scribbled it out and wrote down *MAGNOLIA* in its place.

Once the books were sorted, they had to set the tables right. Since it was almost time for their classes to begin after an elongated circle time period (CTP) that was allotted to all classes, the students hastily arranged themselves into rows & columns of individual tables.

Through the course of the day and the next, the students met all of their subject teachers who enquired about their vacations. They also briefed the students about what they were to learn throughout the year and the type of behaviour that was expected from them during their classes.

The school then closed for a long weekend for it was Independence Day, after the much eventful first 2 days of school.

CHAPTER TWO

THE TROUBLEMAKERS

This batch of students was said to be one of the most – probably even *the* most – notorious batch of the school. They were famous for bullying. The funny thing is that the victims of Magnolian bullying were not always students, in fact, they were mostly teachers!

The act of calling people names behind their backs and bad-mouthing them to others was almost characteristic to the students of Magnolia, with exceptions of course. There was not a single teacher without a nasty nickname and not a single day went by without the coordinator, Ms Elizabeth, having to come to the classroom to warn the students to behave well.

She would walk in and say, "Children, if you do not behave, I will hold you back during your P.E. class," and at the mere mention of that, all the boys would get to quietening the class down so as to prevent themselves from missing their P.E. classes which they loved ever so much. On the contrary, all the girls who detested P.E. classes would intentionally misbehave so as to get the class into detention and to stay back from P.E. classes.

Furthermore, there was much competition with the other section in the grade: Cypress. Most Magnolians wished for them to be ahead of the other section in academics, portion completion, sports, extra-curricular activities and the like. This year, however much Magnolia was troublesome and notorious, the other section was worse – as said by the teachers. At this, all the Magnolians would feel an acute sense of pleasure and a broad smile would show up on their faces.

Ever since Ms Elizabeth had said that there would be awards for the Best Class of Middle School every month, Magnolia wished to get the award. However, they were not very determined in achieving it until the class representative elections, where it was used as a campaigning point.

CHAPTER THREE

Class Rep. Elections

While some genuinely wished to serve the class by helping with its betterment and bridging the gap between students & teachers, most of the candidates that stood for the Class Rep. elections probably wished for the badge that they received for their post. The previous academic year, the class representatives received a badge with their names embossed on it in upper case beside the school logo and their post mentioned below. Hoping for a similar badge this year as well, many ran for the post of class representative.

However, there was a process to it. The process involved first requesting Ms Lancy for permission to run for the post. Only once she gave a go-ahead were they permitted to canvass. Some of the candidates who approached Ms Lancy included Jake, Eleanor, Harry, Margaret, Sophie, Oliver, Holly and some other students. As part of their campaign, the students were allowed to make posters or props to help them canvass. They were, however, encouraged to do so using recyclable materials so as to adhere to the school's annual theme of sustainability.

Thereafter, many of the students began to campaign. While students like Oliver and Holly made posters, students like Sophie made a bookmark out of recycled paper that stated 7 reasons why she should be voted as class representative. Likewise, Margaret cut paper into the shape of a 'T' and wrote on it: **United We Stand**. She also took a picture of her holding it and sent it to everyone by mail the night before the elections took place.

Holly's poster, however, was disapproved by Ms Lancy. This was because she mocked her fellow candidates by morphing their photographs and adding moustaches to them. She was luckily permitted to continue standing for class representative although she was instructed to immediately take down the poster.

The elections were scheduled for the 14th of the month when the class timetable had a CTP class and a Library class, and the results were supposed to be declared the next morning during Ms Lancy's English Language class. Each student of the class, including the candidates, were permitted to vote for 2 candidates by writing down their names on a small piece of paper that would be given by Ms Lancy. The candidates were also permitted to vote for themselves if they wished to.

During the week of the elections, canvassing was in full swing. The candidates went about giving false promises to people. For instance, many promised to bring chocolates, candies and gum to school once a week for everyone. Similarly, many candidates went about telling one another that they would vote the latter if the latter voted for them. This was primarily done by Eleanor. However, these were solely faulty means of getting votes – in short, bribing.

On the day of the elections, all the candidates were dressed in their best. Each one's hair was neatly combed, their nails clipped, they were bathed in perfume and their shirts well ironed with not a speck of dust on them.

While some students spoke off their respective scripts, others kept a tiny notepad in their hands with speech notes. Listening to the students' speeches, it was an almost amusing affair. Some of the students' speeches ran thus:

<u>Eleanor:</u>

"Hello everyone. Today I am running for class representative for one main reason. My mother promised me that if I win the class rep. elections, she would give me an extra 2 hours of TV time. And that is why I stand before you all today. Please vote me as your class rep, so that I can get more TV time."

<u>Jake:</u>

"Hello everyone. I am Jake Morton, and today, I stand before you as a candidate for the post of the class representative of Magnolia. If I win, I promise to bring about change in the class and to bring out the best in everyone. I will work hard towards winning us the Best Class Award, and I promise to help all the students & teachers. Best of luck to my fellow candidates."

<u>Sophie:</u>

"Hi everyone. My name is Sophie, and I am running for class rep of Magnolia. Now, why should you vote for me as your representative? Firstly, I was class rep even last year. Secondly, I have many good qualities. Some are that I am kind, generous, honest, smart, sporty and helpful. I have won many inter-school swimming competitions and am part of the school basketball team. I also got 49/50 in my physics paper last year and 77/80 in mathematics. Therefore, I believe I am the perfect candidate to be your class rep. I hope you consider voting me!"

<u>Harry:</u>

"Hello everyone. Today, I shall not speak much. Do you see this paper aeroplane here in my hand? This has all the goals that I wish to accomplish as class representative of the Magnolia class."

As he showed the sheet, everyone read it carefully. Once everyone was done, he threw the paper aeroplane across the classroom. Surprisingly, due to the direction of air from the ceiling fans, the aeroplane took a perfect round and returned to Harry's hands! Everyone cheered in amusement.

<u>Margaret:</u>

Before beginning her speech, Margaret took a marker and wrote down the following on the whiteboard –

Unity

Safety

Progress

She also took this moment to calm her nerves and take deep breaths while also assessing the mood of the crowd before she commenced her speech.

"Good morning, Magnolia! I'm not going to introduce myself as you guys already know me. However, before I start my speech, I would like to give a fun fact about myself. Did you know that I am a Nobel laureate? Can you guess what I got the Nobel Prize for?"

At this, different people cried "Physics!" or "Space Science!" or "Astronomy!" However, Margaret simply giggled.

"Well, nice guesses, but they are all incorrect. Shall I tell you what I got the prize for?"

Everyone listened eagerly.

"I got the award for making *the BEST* jokes in the world!... That was a joke, you may laugh."

Everyone burst out laughing, well understanding the meaning of her joke. It was not a hidden fact that Margaret could not make any jokes that were worth laughing at. Her jokes would always be science related, making people snap at her in annoyance instead of laugh.

"Jokes apart, let me begin my speech now. I would like to state that I do not stand for this post just for the badge or for the power & authority that come with it. As someone once said, 'with great power comes great responsibility'. Hence, I stand for this post as I believe I would like to serve this class for its betterment. It is prudent for students and teachers to have a good rapport and a free attitude with no restrictions whatsoever. As a strong believer of this, I promise to help my fellow peers and teachers whenever, wherever and however they may need me. I am no superhuman, and hence naturally, I have my own limitations. However, I promise to give you my level best.

If elected, I would like to proceed with this USP that I have written on the board. USP, in business, stands for '*Unique Selling Proposition*'. For me, it is nothing but *Unity, Safety* and *Progress*. As my campaign poster that is hanging on that wall there says, 'United We Stand', without unity, we cannot progress. However, we also need to progress safely to prevent any mishaps or discomfort.

Furthermore, this entire world primarily stands with the support of two pillars: peace and love. Without these, the world will be nothing short of wars, which take place when language fails. Our love for one another is the most important and direct way to be the best class that we wish to be. Like they say, 'We are made of stars. Our teeth have the same calcium that they do, our blood has the same iron that they do, our stomachs have the hydrogen that they do.' Therefore, if we are all made of the same thing, does that not increase the need to be more connected and loving?

Finally, I would like to say that we as a class will definitely work towards winning the *Best Class Award* that we all eye. Although we do not say it, we all definitely want it. Hence, in order to win it, we must be in it together. We need not prove anything to anyone. We need not prove that we are better than Cypress. We are already the best. We are simply yet to be recognised.

I would like to end my speech by saying that even if I am not elected as class rep, I will not cease to help my peers & teachers.

I truly thank you for your time, and best of luck to my fellow candidates."

Once all the speeches were over, the class was given a moment wherein they were meant to write down whom they wished to elect as their two class representatives. They wrote the names down in a piece of paper that Ms Lancy gave them and neatly folded them before submitting them to Ms Lancy.

Considering that there was a lot of time left for the bell to ring, Ms Lancy decided to do the evaluation right then.

The air was so quiet and tense that it could have been cut crisp with a knife. Even the slightest movement or sound would alert everyone. All the candidates sat with their heads in their cupped hands, trying to keep their pounding hearts from falling out of their mouths.

Finally, Ms Lancy, who was counting the number of votes to each candidate, looked up with a grin on her face. As she did, all the students looked at her with anxious faces, the candidates also with a tinge of worry.

Ms Lancy stood up and began to speak. "So, before I tell you the results of the elections, I am going to tell you a story." At this, all the students groaned as they were eager to know who their class representatives were. One candidate even said, "Miss, can you not tell us the story after you tell us who won? My anxiety is kicking in real bad." Ms Lancy replied saying, "Sorry, but you're going to have to wait." The candidates groaned in unison and then chuckled.

"Quiet down, please. Alright. Now that I have your attention, let me tell you that this election was really close. Almost everyone got similar votes, and your two class representatives tied with the number of votes they got. I trust that you voted responsibly and not just for your friends. Anyhow, I have the results in my hands. I'm not going to announce the individual votes. If you wish to know how much you got, you can come up to me and ask. Coming to the winners, they are..........." There was a long dramatic pause wherein the candidates sat solemnly with their hands folded and eyes closed.

CHAPTER FOUR

THE WINNER IS...

"Your first class rep. is......Jake Morton!!!!!" announced Ms Lancy, finally. The class burst into a brief applause as Jake walked up to the front of the class before quieting down to hear the name of their second class rep.

"As I said before, this was a tie between Jake and.........Ms Margaret!!!!" exclaimed Ms Lancy. The process repeated: the class burst into an applause as Margaret walked up to the front of the class. Ms Lancy then said, "Would our newly elected class representatives like to tell us something?"

While Jake thanked the class for their votes, Margaret said, "I am truly grateful to all of you for placing your trust in me and my fellow class representative. Honestly, I really did not expect winning this." The class once again broke into an applause.

"Alright, alright," said Ms Lancy. "Now that you guys have two class reps, you must approach them for anything you need. And as class reps, you have to help out the teachers whenever asked as well. I want my class to win the Best Class Award, and you will do so by listening to your class representatives, alright?" "YES, MISS!!" exclaimed the class in unison.

However, life as a class rep was not always easy – especially for Margaret. Margaret was bold and strategic, but did not have a voice loud enough to grab everyone's attention. Besides, Jake, who was supposed to help Margaret bring an end to all the misbehaviour, agreed that there was no harm in having some fun.

Nevertheless, the class ran just fine with Jake and Margaret running around and down the corridors, trying their best to 'tame' the class.

CHAPTER FIVE

MANI VENKATESH

A few months into their school year, the Magnolian students wrote their mid-term exams that was called *Unit Test 1*. These assessments happened right after the Dussehra holidays and ended a week before the Diwali holidays commenced, before which they had their parent-teacher meeting. Preceding that, however, were the paper discussions for their test papers.

The day the students' assessments ended, they were relaxed and chilling in their classroom. They were goofing around, making disturbing noises and running about, rejoicing at the termination of their 'headache'. That was when they spotted a little beige-coloured object peep out from underneath the digital clock that hung high up in the ceiling of the wall on which the whiteboard and the projector screen were attached.

As the students slowly crept towards the wall, they found that the beige object was moving. When they banged the wall, everyone jerked backwards at the sight of a lizard! It was a fully grown massive lizard with black beady eyes that perked up and down alertly. While some students ran out the door screaming their lungs out, the others stayed in and marvelled at the lizard whom they soon began to form a bond with.

The next day, all the students walked into the class and took their seats mechanically, forgetting what they had seen the previous afternoon. That was when the massive lizard peeped out from the back of the clock again.

"Hey look! It's Mani Venkatesh!" cried an excited student, pointing at the lizard.

"WHO?!?!" exclaimed the other perplexed students.

"That's Mani Venkatesh. He is to be our class pet. We have named it Mani Venkatesh," explained another student. "Now that's slayyyy," cried another student in the class.

Through the course of the final 2 days before school closed for Diwali, all the teachers were introduced to Mani Venkatesh. While some took it as a joke and ignored it, other extremely terrified teachers refused to come to the front of the class; an example being Ms Lancy.

While the joke of the 'class pet' ensued, the students were also quite disheartened by their test results. Right before they got their geography papers, everyone raged at their teacher, Ms Anne, complaining about the paper having questions related to topics that were not taught to them. However, when they received their papers, they were satisfied with the splendid marks that they never expected to obtain.

Likewise, there was a big commotion as to who had got the highest in each subject. As a result of the exam results, Thomas and Margaret were stamped as the 'Class Geniuses', considering their marks. However, Margaret continued to remind everyone that each individual has their own strengths and weaknesses. "Those who may be good at academics need not be good at sports or arts and vice-versa," she said. However, the class solely considered this as her modesty and continued to call her the 'Class

Genius', much to her discontent.

Meanwhile, the class continued to make up a life story for their class pet, Mani Venkatesh, the lizard.

Many teachers did find the whole concept very questionable. For instance, the biology teacher (Ms Fernandes) asked the class, "How do you know the gender of the lizard?" At this, Jamie replied saying, "Miss, we do not know its gender. That is why the name is *Mani*, which is a unisex name." She then asked, "Isn't Venkatesh the name of a God? Why then have you given it to a lizard?" At this, Jamie again said, "Miss, we just wanted to make the name funny & unique."

CHAPTER SIX

THE STAY-BACK DRAMA

One Tuesday, when Magnolia had to have a math lesson, Ms Elizabeth told them that their teacher, Ms Hendricks, was absent. The moment she stepped out of the classroom, almost everyone in the class screamed euphorically. At that moment, Ms Elizabeth returned. She said, "I warn you guys. If anything happens, I will hold you back from your P.E. class." Almost instantaneously, the entire class fell silent.

In a few moments, however, the class was up and joyful again. After all, their math teacher was absent, and they had two free sessions for they had 2 math lessons on Tuesdays. Moreover, they also had a block period of P.E., making the day more exciting for some.

The class was a commotion. Everyone screeched and ran about the class hysterically, playing tag and hitting one another with books. This was primarily by people like Alice, Hannah, Lewis, Adam, Ben, Oliver, Samuel, Jamie, Luke, Jake and Stacy. The others, although not sitting idle, did not run about the entire classroom in a manic fashion. Instead, they sat in their seats and gossiped. This included people like Laura, Eleanor, Sophie and Amy. Holly, on the other hand, was drawing in her scrapbook and making trinkets out of beads. She was running a small-time business for which she was advertising by doing so. Amber, in the meantime, simply sat and took in all that was happening, laughing and occasionally talking to Margaret when she sat down exhausted after screaming at the class, trying in vain to quieten them down. The thing with Margaret was that her so called 'screaming' was not really to the Magnolian standards. Her scream was what any other Magnolian would call a whisper. Therefore, she was helpless. Moreover, her loud fellow class rep. was busy wrecking an old science project by slamming it loudly against the wall a thousand times until it shattered into innumerable pieces of broken wood.

"Guys! Please quiet down! If Ms Elizabeth or any other teacher hears us – which is *very* likely to happen – we will all get into trouble!" said Margaret, 'whispering' her lungs out. "Oh, you're just saying that because you are *Margaret* and you've never gotten into trouble. I'm sure she will burst out into a river of tears if a teacher even raises their voice – whether she made a mistake or not," joked Jake who was in fact supposed to *help* Margaret instead of opposing her. At this, everybody laughed. Rolling her eyes and murmuring to herself in dismay, Margaret returned to her seat.

"You know, I do feel kind of bad for you sometimes," said Amber as her crony, Margaret, sipped some water to soothe her sore throat. Margaret replied, "Oh yes, you should. I try my level best to not get our class into trouble, but it just does not work!" "Well, to me, that sounds like a skill issue," joked Amber. Margaret rolled her eyes at her.

Just then, Oliver started a mob of people who were singing the song, *'I'm a Barbie Girl'*. Most of the class sang the song in perfect tune and in unison, with Luke leading. Amber hurriedly shut the windows that opened into the corridor in order to prevent the escape of the roaring sound that the class made as they sang:

"I'm a Barbie girl, in the Barbie wooorld....life in plastic, it's fantastic!

You can brush my hair, and dress me anywheeeere....imagination, life is your creation!

Come on Barbie, let's go party – oh, oh, oh...

Come on Barbie, let's go party – ooh ooh ooh, ooh ooh ooh......"

The math class was supposed to be from 9:50 AM to 10:35 AM, and it was already around 10:20 AM. Stacy, along with Eleanor & Laura, was swiftly sneaking out of the classroom, careful enough to let out minimum sound, to wander off into the corridors when she saw Ms Elizabeth and Ms Lancy advancing towards them. The three girls instantly rushed back into the classroom to warn the others. When they did, the children hastily returned to their seats, put away their playing cards, threw the gum that they were chewing into the bin and stashed the countless broken pieces of wood behind their non-functional air cooler that lay in the back corner of the classroom behind the wall, all in panic. Margaret awed at how the class worked in unison in times of trouble, lighting an idea in her mind.

Finally, when Ms Elizabeth stormed into the classroom with Ms Lancy striding behind her, the class fell silent. The teachers stood at the front of the classroom, giving the children a truly intimidating silent treatment. The children looked at one another in worry, realising too late of what they had done in the past hour.

"This behaviour is simply unacceptable," began Ms Elizabeth. "You guys are in your second year of Middle School now and yet you behave like kindergarten children. No. Even the children in kindergarten behave better than you. Have you seen how they *quietly* walk in a single straight line to their classes? If you have not, it is truly commendable. Do you even know how loud you were? I could hear you all the way down in my office. And where is my office? Halfway down the corridor." She paused to give a look at everyone. She then continued, "Did you know? Although I sit right next to a fifth-grade classroom, I never get the slightest sound from there and never have to complain about reducing their sound levels during my meetings. Moreover, you guys should consider the fact that there is a meeting that the Head of School, Ms Victoria, is having with some parents right down there in the AV room."

The children exchanged glances of guilt as Ms Elizabeth continued to speak, Ms Lancy looking at her class in disillusion – she definitely expected *much* better behaviour from her children.

Ms Elizabeth then screamed, "Who are the class reps? Please come here." Jake and Margaret got up and walked towards their section coordinator, their hearts pounding and their legs trembling as they advanced forward. Amber looked solemnly at her friend who was most likely to get scolded at.

"As class representatives, you both are in charge of the class. Thus, it is your prime responsibility to make sure the class is disciplined and in order. What were the two of you doing when the class was in commotion?" At this, Jake tried to speak, "Miss...uhh....we...umm... we actually..." Seeing that Jake was unable to speak out the truth, Ms

Elizabeth said, "Alright, alright. Maybe you might say that this unruly behaviour was too much for you to handle. In that case, you should have at least called some teacher! Firstly, a class is not *supposed* to be left unsupervised. Therefore, I do not know why you people do not have a substitute teacher to supervise you. Do not shrug at me, Jake! As class reps, you should have gone downstairs to the reception and asked the teacher there to send a teacher to the class." As she said this, Margaret's eyes began to fill with tears. Seeing this, Ms Elizabeth took a deep breath and continued softly.

"Look, children. This behaviour is nothing short of unacceptable. I have priorly forgiven you many times for your misbehaviour but unfortunately cannot do so henceforth. If I do, you will continue this behaviour and no change will be brought about. As your teacher, it is my utmost duty to discipline you so that you grow up to be splendid citizens of the world. Therefore, I will have to detain you from P.E."

At this, there was an uproar from most of the students (except Amber, Margaret, Eleanor, Laura, Amy and Adam for they did not like P.E. as much – at all). Surely, they did not want to miss out on a moment of their P.E. classes! Hence, Alice pleaded to Ms Elizabeth, "Miss, please, Ms Elizabeth! We promise never to misbehave! Please let us go for P.E. Already, we are quite exhausted from our assessments and haven't got any time to go outdoors and play. Please, Ms Elizabeth! We promise you that we will silently do math during our next free class. Please, Miss! Please!" Her pleads were quite of the appealing type, but nothing could cause Ms Elizabeth to waver. She firmly replied, "You kids will sit in here – *quietly* – under the supervision of Ms Lancy. Thereafter, if she feels that you children have become calm enough and will not cause any more trouble, she will let you go for P.E. The bus will be awaiting you at the gate." Saying this, Ms Elizabeth left the classroom, and Margaret & Jake returned to their seats silently.

The next hour, they spent in silence. Occasionally, if somebody whispered loudly enough to make Ms Lancy raise her head, the entire class would bark them into silence. Not a soul dared to talk. Ms Lancy sat at the teachers' table, silently correcting papers. She was unhappy with her students' behaviour and was now almost sure that they would not win the Best Class Award. So much so, she did not even look them in the eye.

Finally, Eleanor got annoyed with all the silence and discipline. She began talking to Laura, who was sitting beside her, loudly. Luke, Alice, Jake and some others tried to silence her but in vain. She listened to nobody. Annoyed, Alice finally burst out saying, "Eleanor! *We* did this, and hence, *we* have to face the consequences. Now, we must compensate for our mistakes by at least staying quiet for two hours so that we can go for P.E. at least next week if not this week. Is that so much to ask?" At this, Eleanor nodded and smirked in a way that annoyed Alice even further. "Fine. If you do not want to go for P.E., that is completely alright. At least stay silent so that we can all go for P.E., and then, you can do what you want and gossip your heart out with Laura on the field." Although very offended at this comment, Eleanor remained silent thereafter. Ms Lancy, witnessing all that was happening until now, looked up at the clock hanging high up on the wall behind her. She then opened her phone and dialled a number. A moment later, she covered her mouth with her hand, as if she were whispering, and spoke softly so that only the children seated in front of her – Amber and Margaret – could hear what she said.

"Elizabeth, the kids have been behaving well for the past forty minutes. Shall I let them go?" After listening carefully to the instructions that her coordinator gave her, Ms Lancy put down the phone and looked up at the children who were looking at her intently with a blue desire. She smiled. She then slowly began to put away her papers and stationery, picked up her phone and then stood up. She smiled again. Then, she said, "I was indeed disappointed when I heard of your behaviour and Ms Elizabeth shouting at you. I know that not everyone did this, but everyone had to suffer. You'll understand when you grow up a little more that that's just how life is! Unfair."

At this, everyone exchanged confused glances. "Anyway, the past hour has been really peaceful in this class. You all behaved commendably well, and I liked the fact that you all realised and accepted your mistakes. I was really upset at your behaviour at first, but now I am truly proud of you for this as well." The children smiled at each other and at their teacher, who smiled back at them. "As Ms Elizabeth said, "The bus will be awaiting you at the gate.""

The children were not yet completely sure whether that was permission to leave or was an implied indication that the bus *would* be waiting for them the next time they left for their P.E. class. Alice looked at Ms Lancy. Almost as if reading her thoughts, Ms Lancy smiled and nodded. Alice jumped up and screamed, "WE CAN GO!!!!!"

After a moment of silence, there was a terrible uproar. Everyone grabbed their water bottles and ran out of the class at top speed as if they were a military regiment, ready to take on their rivals. Ms Lancy ran after them, screaming across the corridor, "Please be on your best behaviour, lest you should be detained again!" Ms Lancy then went back to the staff room, laughing.

The Magnolian children were mocked at by those from Cypress for they had been detained and had missed a P.E. class for their misbehaviour. Thus, it was established that Cypress was a better and more well-behaved class. However, the return for this bullying was to be faced by the children of Cypress very soon in the academic year.

CHAPTER SEVEN

A 40-Minute Speech

The next day, the children had gotten over the fact that they had been detained from P.E. and were happy that no more P.E. classes had to be missed that day, when they had another block period of P.E. class. They were, however, scolded at by Ms Hendricks – their math teacher.

On Thursday, during the next math class (for there was no math or science on Wednesdays, as per the timetable of Magnolia) after their detention, Ms Hendricks walked in rather upset.

"Count of ten and I want everyone in their places," she exclaimed as she entered the classroom, counting backwards from ten. She stopped counting at three when she saw that everyone had settled. She set down her books on the table and let her weight be carried by her hands that were resting on the teacher's chair. She looked rather intimidatingly at her students, making eye contact with one student and then another.

"I had prepared a worksheet for you and assigned it to a teacher who was supposed to be your substitute. I do not make worksheets *just* because it's my job to do so. In fact, it is *not* my job to make worksheets. Do you know how much effort goes into making these worksheets? Besides, I do not benefit at all by doing this. Although you find it torturous at this stage in life, it will highly benefit you when you grow up. I am doing this because *your* future is at stake. If the substitute whom I had assigned was absent, it is your duty to ask for another," said Ms Hendricks. She paused. She glanced at all of her students who had a look of guilt on their faces. She sighed and said, "Alright. Now there is no point in wasting time by talking about the past. You got your detention, and you have learned your lesson. Now let's get on with math. Since you did not do the worksheet that day, I am going to give it to you today as homework." Unlike usually, the children did not complain about getting homework this time for *they* were to blame in this case. "If the homework is not done by tomorrow, I promise to give you another detention from *my* side. You will not go for P.E. classes next week as well. Is that understood?" The children nodded in agreement quietly, before taking out their notebooks to do math sums.

By now, the unfortunate occurrence of the previous week was almost forgotten. The children had moved on from all the penalising that they faced, both from most teachers, who threatened them with detention, and the children from Cypress, who had almost officially established that they were the better class.

The next Tuesday, Ms Hendricks had to invigilate for the eleventh-grade board exams. Thus, the children had yet another free period. Just as the children were about to run out onto the school football ground to play, Margaret asked Jake to get her everyone's attention for a few minutes.

"EVERYONE SHUT UP & SIT DOWN FOR SOME TIME. MARGARET WANTS TO TALK," screamed Jake in such a deafening volume that Margaret had to press her hands to her ears. Although groaning, all the Magnolians returned to their seats while Margaret swiftly fetched a tiny notepad from the front pocket of her school bag. She then took her place behind the teacher's table and waited for everyone to settle down.

"Why do you wish to hold us back when we have a free period? We want to play!" said Luke to Margaret in a rather defying manner. "I am terribly apologetic for the inconvenience caused by me, but I will take only five minutes of your time. Thereafter, you can leave for the ground," said Margaret calmly. At this, everyone quietened and listened to her, trying to push back their impatience to go play.

"Many weeks ago," she began, "I stood at this very spot and delivered a speech as a candidate for the post of class rep. Moments later, I delivered yet another brief speech *as* the elected class representative of this wonderful, wonderful class – Magnolia. During both the speeches, I mentioned some of the goals that I would like to achieve as class rep. I believe I have, hitherto, succeeded in most. However, I have very eminently failed to achieve one of those goals: for us to achieve the Best Class Award." She looked around at everyone in the class, who surprisingly listened quietly. She then took a brief look at her notepad and then continued, "I have in fact been awaiting this opportunity for a long while now. I wish to share some things with you that I feel are quintessential for us to become a better class.

Did you know, one such Tuesday, when some of the younger students of Middle School were waiting outside our class for us to leave so that they could enter for their after-school CAS club, many of us began singing *I'm a*

Barbie Girl. Finally, when some of the kids entered the classroom because they were tired of waiting outside, I told them to ignore us because we are a little cuckoo banana bread. At this, do you know what one of them said? She said, 'I hope our batch doesn't become like yours.' At that moment I smiled at her, but that comment was a punch in the gut. We, as one of the elder batches of Middle School, are supposed to be role models for our juniors. However, I don't think we are worthy of that honour, considering our current behaviour. I have complete belief that each and every one of us present here has the potential to be someone our youngsters can look up to. All that is required is a little bit of polishing.

Last year as well, the class that I was in was *THE* most notorious batch of the entire school – not just Middle School. Those who were with me last year may remember that we did all sorts of things: many people were on the verge of getting detention, our class rep was forced to vacate her post and was replaced after many months of deliberation, we broke a piano in the music room and much more. However, not once did Ms Elizabeth actually give us a detention. This year, we have not been nearly as 'bad' as we were last year, but have got into detention – definitely not good! And the thing is, our class is just so talented and smart that I do not think we *deserve* to get into trouble.

Therefore, in order to win Best Class, not get into trouble and be a role model for our juniors, all we must do is control our behaviour a little. For instance, maybe we could stop screaming across the corridor or stop wrecking things in & around the classroom."

At this moment, while Margaret was completely engrossed in delivering her speech (now off-the-cuff and without her little notepad) and the others in listening to it, some students sneaked out of the classroom to roam around the corridors. These students were Eleanor, Laura and Stacy. However, nobody noticed this.

"Furthermore," continued Margaret, "if we wish to win the Best Class Award, we could also maybe re-organise our class a little bit; probably clean up the floors, arrange the tables & chairs in neat rows and columns and the like. We could also put together some of the talents that our fellow classmates have to better the class. For instance, Holly could suggest – and if possible, even bring – some good plant types that may help beautify our classroom. If these plants are maintenance-free, that would be wonderful! Another idea was one that I had thought of at the very beginning of the year, when Ms Lancy asked us to come up with some good ideas to decorate the classroom. Since that space at the back behind the wall cannot be used for seating for the students cannot see the teachers and vice-versa, I thought we could probably make it a nice reading nook. We could add a beanbag and make a rug out of 23 pieces of scrap cloth – one from each Magnolian. Then somebody, who is interested and/or can stitch, may stitch all of these together into a rectangular shape to make it a rug or a carpet. In addition, we could empty all of that scrap from the shelf there that have accumulated over the years, and we can all donate a book – or few books – each. Thus, we could read during our free periods or lunchtime. Again, since this is *our* class, *we* are responsible for it."

"Excuse me, Margaret, but you said that you would take 'five minutes of our time', but it has already been half an hour since you said that. Can we go to the ground at least now?" asked an impatient Luke. "Guys, Margaret is trying to take an initiative for the betterment of Magnolia and of all Magnolians. Why don't you guys silently listen to her?" said Ben, much to everyone's shock for he was one of the children that always defied Margaret. "Why, thank you, Ben," said a surprised Margaret. Right at that moment, the trio that went wandering off into the corridors returned to the class. When enquired, they were speechless. However, Margaret did not bother to take the matter forward. She simply told them to take their seats.

"I am truly sorry for taking up your time, but I really felt that this little talk was necessary. The point of all this is simply that we can be *much* better than we currently are if we wish to," said Margaret. At this, Eleanor said, "Oh yeah, I totally agree. Did anyone else notice that Margaret was able to control the class really easily for almost 35 minutes now when not a single teacher so far has been able to do so?" "OH YEAHHH," said everyone in unison. Margaret smiled. She then continued to speak.

"I know this was not supposed to be for so long. However, I believe this was long overdue. I know that the next thing you are going to ask me is whether we can go early for P.E. However, my answer is sadly going to be 'no', for I do not have the authority to leave the class early or late – that authority is solely with our teachers. Now, I would like to open up this forum for everybody. Do you have any ideas? Any suggestions? Something that can help make our class better?"

As soon as Margaret asked this question, everyone began to shoot suggestions at her, teeming with ideas. Soon after, when they had to line up for P.E., everyone stood in a single line – this showed that they were truly impacted by the speech. This discipline, to everyone's surprise, continued for the rest of the day.

Right after lunch, the Magnolians had their physics lesson. Their teacher, Mr Richard, was a rather fun-loving and carefree person. Cracking jokes, passing sarcastic comments on everyone and roasting everyone around him were almost characteristic to him. The students took much advantage of this, insulting and roasting him back. However, Mr Richard dealt with them well by giving them a dose of their own medicine. Magnolia was much noisier and entropic than usual during their physics lessons due to the same.

However, this one day, even Mr Richard felt a change in their behaviour. He tolerated it for a while but then could just not resist asking. Hence, he said in a rather confused tone, "What is it with you people today, huh? What happened to all the noise and chaos that usually ensues during my classes? Nobody is back answering me today; nobody is screaming at the top of their voice; not many people came late today; your class is smelling *much* better than it usually does; your class looks much neater than it usually is – there is no paper on the floor and the whiteboard is wiped clean, ready for me to write on. What really happened?" At this, Luke replied, "Sir, you can ask that to Margaret yourself. She will tell you." Everyone chuckled at this, but Mr Richard enquired with Margaret. In return, she said, "Well, sir, that's because the class listened to a forty-minute speech today."

Even more confused than before, he asked, "*A FORTY-MINUTE SPEECH?* By whom?" At this, everyone pointed at Margaret. He then said, "How did you speak for forty minutes, Margaret? Rather, *what* could you speak about for so long?" Margaret replied smilingly, "I was talking about how each individual in the class has the potential to become a role model for our juniors and that we as a class are capable of winning the Best Class Award – with a little tweak." Mr Richard blinked blankly at Margaret, trying to fathom what she had just said and the effect that it had caused. Before he could say anything else, Eleanor intervened, saying, "And did you know, sir? She managed to keep the class quietly listening to her throughout her speech!"

Mr Richard then spoke, now more amused than confused, "WOW! I don't suppose a teacher has been able to do that with your class either, right?" Everyone nodded in agreement. "Wait a minute – is that why Margaret was standing at the teacher's table during the third or fourth period?" "Yes. Very much, sir. She bored me to death! But her speech was indeed true and definitely very effective," said Luke. "Oh yes, that is very eminently visible," said Mr Richard.

The effect of the speech was carry-forwarded during the last lesson as well, which was mathematics. Ms Hendricks, just like Mr Richard, was truly very amused at the Magnolian children behaving so well.

However, as Margaret had expected and Amber had predicted, all the discipline that the Magnolians followed was very short-lived. The next morning, they were back to all of their usual activity – screaming, swearing and wrecking. "Well, at least they listened for one day!" said Margaret to Amber, sighing as Amber chuckled. "Skill issue," she thereafter said to Margaret.

CHAPTER EIGHT

Naughty Students, Naughtier Teachers

There is a very common statement by most parents to their children and by many teachers to their students. It runs thus: *"If you think you are smart, do not forget that I am smarter."* Likewise, the teachers teaching Magnolia have a similar statement: *"If you think you are naughty, do not forget that I am naughtier."* There have been many incidents that have proved their statement right.

One such incident occurred during a Magnolian mathematics lesson. When someone in the class announced that Ms Hendricks was on her way to class, Oliver walked out of the class. Suddenly, he came in screaming, "Count of ten and I want everybody in your places!" Just then, Ms Hendricks entered the door and saw Oliver. In contrary to what the class had expected, scolds, Ms Hendricks simply smiled and walked up to the front of the class where Oliver was. She then asked him, "Were you mimicking me when you said that?" "No, Miss. I was not mimicking you. I was simply enacting how you usually enter the class every day." At this, the entire class, including Ms Hendricks, burst out laughing. "I see. How else can you enact me?" asked Ms Hendricks, in a very jolly mood. "Hold on, Miss. Let me show you." Saying this, Oliver cleared his throat. He then began: "Luke! Get up, get out!" Yet again, the entire class burst into a thousand laughs.

Ms Hendricks, much to everyone's surprise, thereafter said, "Now that you people mocked me, let *me* mock *you*." Everyone cheered her and clapped as she began enacting the character of all those who mocked her/back-answered her time and again.

"This is Adam: '*Miss, is my handwriting alright?*' Trust me, the sweet boy asks me this almost every day. And every time, I tell him yes.

Okay next, this is Luke: '*Ms Hendricks, you are going too slow! Everybody has finished and here we are waiting for one kid who has not finished!*'"

"Ms Hendricks, what can you do for Margaret?" asked Luke, smirking. "Well, what *can* I do for Margaret? She is always quiet in the class and does whatever I tell her to. All I can do for her is this," and Ms Hendricks sat down on the teacher's chair and pretended to write in her book. Although this was not nearly as hilarious as the other acts she performed, this act received the maximum amount of laughter.

Another instance was with Mr Bill, the history teacher. Mr Bill, for a very unknown reason, had a liking towards making jokes (sometimes lame ones) and comments related to explosive diarrhoea.

One such joke was on Halloween. Halloween was celebrated with full pomp in this school, and hence, everyone (including teachers) was encouraged to wear Halloween costumes to school on that day. Although the Elementary School teachers were more festive and creepy, the Middle & High School teachers were not all boring either! Many wore scary make-up and some even wore whacky costumes. The students, on the other hand, celebrated Halloween in full swing! They wore wigs, brought props and were clad in the scariest of Halloween costumes. Yet, there were exceptions – some being Margaret, Amber, Daniel and some more. While Margaret and Amber were simply clad in black, Daniel came to school in his school uniform!

Jamie was one of the children who brought props to school. His prop was a rubber forearm that had blood oozing from the area of the elbow joint which looked like it was ripped apart from the rest of the arm, for there was presence of flesh & a piece of bone – all covered in blood.

When Mr Bill entered the classroom, the first thing he saw was the rubber forearm. When Jamie whispered to him that Margaret was getting disgusted by the look of the bleeding flesh & bone, Mr Bill ran towards her with the arm in his hand and shoved it in her face. While she shrieked in fear, mostly out of empathy for the person whose arm it may have been (although it was of rubber), the rest of the class had a good laugh. Next, Eleanor came up to Mr Bill to show him her costume. After praising her creativity, Mr Bill wiped the rubber arm on the floor and then placed it on her head saying, "Here, I am sweeping explosive diarrhoea from the floor, and now, I am going to wipe it on your head." He then began laughing as Eleanor made a disgusted expression.

Another instance where he joked about explosive diarrhoea was on the first day of school after the Christmas holidays. Mr Bill asked Amy about what she did during her winter break. She said, "Sir, I did nothing except play video games and go to Margaret's house." At this, Margaret said, "Did you know, sir? When she came home, I fed her a choco-lava cake, and she thereafter went high on sugar!" In return, Mr Bill said, "Amy, I hope you did not spoil Margaret's bathrooms after eating all those cakes and getting explosive diarrhoea!"

One Monday, Margaret was absent to school as she was under the weather. Although only one student was absent, the entire class – including the teachers – faced a big problem: there were no markers or dusters in the class! Since many people were stealing the markers & dusters from both Cypress and Magnolia, Ms Lancy told Margaret to keep the markers and duster with her so as to prevent them from getting stolen. Since this was the first (and only) time Margaret was absent, nobody knew what to do in order to obtain markers and dusters. Furthermore, since both Magnolians and children from Cypress blamed each other for stealing each other's markers, nobody trusted those from the other class and hence did not lend markers or dusters in the fear that they would not be returned.

Later that day, when Mr Richard entered Magnolia during his lesson, he was about to ask for a marker from Margaret when he realised that she was missing. "Oy! What happened to Margaret? Where is she? Is she bunking?" asked Mr Richard, filled with curiosity. "Oh no sir," said Amber. "She's absent." At this, Mr Richard was at first silent, trying to fathom how Margaret could be absent. Almost suddenly, he jumped up, punching the air in joy. "Whoa, sir! What happened?" asked Luke. "I'm so glad she is absent!" said Mr Richard in return, his eyes gleaming like stars. "Sir, I'm going to tell this to Margaret," said Stacy, teasingly. "*Dare* you tattle off to her. Else, be prepared to get a big fat F on your physics paper," said Mr Richard.

The next day, Margaret came back to school. Although she did not run a temperature or have a cold, she had a raspy voice. "Here, here! My lovely friend here has the raspiest voice the world can ever hear! $100 for a ticket to come hear her voice!" exclaimed Amber, teasing Margaret when she first spoke. Margaret simply rolled her eyes at her friend and nodded sideways, smiling. After their first lesson, which was chemistry, Amber and Margaret joined their friends – namely Amy, Sophie, Eleanor, Laura, Stacy and some other girls from Cypress – for breakfast. That was when the beans spilled.

"Margaret, did you know what Mr Richard did yesterday?" asked Stacy with a smirk on her face. "No, what did he do? Did he put moment of force as 'M'? Or did he put force with a lowercase 'f'?" asked Margaret. "No, silly," said Amber, predicting the upcoming situation. "Well, when we told him that you were absent, he jumped up in joy," said Stacy, closely observing Margaret's expression. "Oh," said Margaret, not expecting that even in her wildest dreams. "Not only that, he also punched his hand in the air and said 'Yes! I'm so glad she's absent!'" said Amy. "Well...I mean, that's his opinion," said Margaret calmly, much contradicting the expression that all the girls expected to see. "And here I was thinking she'll do a typical noir-et-blanche movie heroine expression of grief," said Amy, rolling her eyes. Margaret smiled naughtily at her disappointed friends, thoroughly enjoying the expressions on their faces.

CHAPTER NINE

LOCKED IN A BATHROOM!

P.E. class was the one class that had contradicting feelings among students; while some loved it with all their heart, others strongly detested it. So much so, the ones who loved it would beg for free periods so that they could go play sports, while the ones who did not would stoop to any level in order to bunk P.E. lessons.

For many, playing sports was not what they did not like – it was playing in the sun that they hated, an example being Margaret. For many others, both were problematic, an example being Amber. Thus, somewhere in late October, the two cronies formulated a plan to skip their P.E. lesson – they intended to stay in the washroom throughout the entire block period. Usually, Margaret was a rule-abiding pupil. However, she took this P.E. lesson as an exception; the sole reason for this was that it was a free lesson with all but one of the P.E. teachers gone with students for inter-school competitions. Hence, the day's P.E. lesson was anyway to be less eventful and almost a free period.

Since the school football & basketball courts were not very big, another arena – by the name of Paddington –

was used by the school for sports lessons. The arena was exclusively for the students of the school and was located in a by-lane of the school building; hence, transporting the students was untroublesome, a bus ride taking less than 5 minutes. The arena had facilities for football, basketball, throwball/volleyball, cricket and even swimming. As huge an area as it was, the arena had minimal tree cover, making the scorching sun much too undesired to play in.

The arena also had a washroom, which was nothing more than a small shed-like structure with a separation for the male and female restrooms. The female restroom had two wash-basins and three compartments – two lavatories on either side of a bathing area. Since it would be unusual for two girls to be locked up in one lavatory for over three quarters of an hour, the girls decided to lock themselves inside the sparsely used bathing compartment.

The moment the bus carrying the Magnolians arrived at Paddington, the girls kept their bottles near the back wall of the washroom building and picked up a basketball each and dribbled away for almost half an hour, subtly planning their secret trip to the washroom. Approximately three quarters of an hour later, after one of the sports lessons of the two was over, the girls subtly took their water bottles and swiftly disappeared from the area. They then placed their bottles on the bottle stand near the front side of the washroom building, meant for the football players. After they were doubly sure that nobody was around watching them, Margaret put on her mask and then gestured to Amber to follow her into the washroom. Once there, they were welcomed by their friends, Amy and Sophie, who were washing their hands at the washbasin.

"Hey!" said Amy as soon as she sighted her friends. "Killing the gangster look, Maggs!" "Hi..." said Amber, looking at Margaret as if hoping for a plan thereafter. Thinking on her feet, Margaret said, "Hi Amy and Sophie! Oh, I always wear my mask inside washrooms, elevators and in crowded areas. Amber, please will you wait here while I use the restroom?" At Amber's nod, she entered one of the lavatories and locked the door. In about a minute, Amy and Sophie were done washing their hands and made their way out of the washroom, waving a noisy 'goodbye' to Amber.

"Psst...Margaret..." whispered Amber, making sure nobody else was in the proximity of the washroom. "You can come out now. They're gone." At this, Margaret quietly unlocked the door and slyly stepped out of the stall. "Phew...that was close!" sighed Margaret, relieved that they were not caught. "I was so frightened seeing them that I was speechless! My mind went blank, and I didn't know what to do," laughed Amber. "Anyway, let us not waste any more time. Let's get into the bathing area. Quick!" Saying this, the two girls scampered into the bathing area and locked the door quietly.

In around ten minutes, as the girls were talking and laughing in amusement at what they had just done, they heard something. Footsteps!

Yet again, Amber went speechless – this time, however, for a good reason. The two girls hushed and watched a shadow pass from the gap beneath the door of the stall. The two girls remained dead-still for around 2 minutes. Then, judging the situation and looking at Amber's constipated expression, Margaret began to chuckle softly. Amber gave her a look of "Shut up unless you want to get caught!" At this, Margaret put her hand over her mask and shut her eyes to prevent herself from bursting out into an air guzzling laughter.

The next moment, they heard a flush and the opening of the latch the moment after that. The girls, Margaret now back to being quiet at the sudden realisation of the dire trouble & offence that could be caused by her laughter, listened quietly at the squeaky turning of a metal that allowed water to gush down the tap and then the sound of it closing almost momentarily. Thereafter, faded footsteps were heard.

Margaret bent down to look from the gap below the door of the stall to see if the person was still there. When she motioned to Amber that the person was gone, Margaret burst out laughing. Suddenly, a loud revving began. The sound was almost as if they were standing inside a motor that rotated at 3000 rpm. In other words, it was deafening!

"WHAT IS THIS SOUND?!?!" exclaimed Amber. "It might be a DG or something. After all, there were frequent power failures all morning," replied Margaret. "What's a DG?!?!" asked Amber, barely hearing what Margaret's soft voice spoke amidst the hammering sound. "Diesel Generator." Not able the bear the sound, the girls grabbed their ears with their palms, trying to block out the noise.

Once the ear-splitting sound stopped, the girls sighed. "Whatever that is, it sure is loud!" said Amber, giggling. "Ouch! My eardrums! It was almost like they were playing a band in my ears!" joked Margaret. At this, the two girls laughed.

"Seriously though, Margaret! What's with you and your unstoppable temptation to laugh!" joked Amber. "No, actually, I do have that problem. Whenever I'm in the lift with my mother and someone else enters, I start laughing as soon as I see anybody else apart from myself. In fact, even if I face the wall, I start chuckling," said Margaret. After looking at one another for a moment, both the girls began giggling.

Once Margaret was finished attending to her cheeks down which rolled tears of laughter, she looked down at her watch. "It's almost time. Only five minutes remaining. Shall we go?" asked Margaret. "Yes. However, we must make sure nobody sees us come out of the washroom together," said Amber. "Of course, of course. We can grab our bottles and quickly go to the water-filling station, pretending to be tired," said Margaret. "Oh yes. After all, you required so much effort to stop sniffling when that person came into the washroom!" joked Amber. After yet another brief session of giggles, Margaret said, "Jokes apart, I will open the door slightly and look out to see if anyone is there. Then, you follow me out, and we shall pretend to wash our hands," explained Margaret. "Yes. However, we cannot exit the washroom at the same time. You exit first, pick up your bottle and proceed to the bottle-filling station. I shall follow you once I've seen that you've passed the washroom and gone to the other side," said Amber. "Good thinking." Thereafter, Margaret slowly undid the latch and peered out through the gap. Seeing that nobody was there, the two girls scampered out and followed their little ruse. Just as they filled their bottles, they boarded their buses totally normally.

CHAPTER TEN

SPORTS DAY

Towards the end of November, the children had their Term End Exams. The results were mostly positive, and Ms Elizabeth assured Magnolia that they were one of the best-performing classes of Middle School.

School was supposed to close for Christmas a week after the exams. The first Saturday of their vacation, 17th December, was Sports Day. Therefore, the week in between the termination of the Term End Exams and Sports Day was to be utilised for paper discussions (two days) and Sports Day practices (all week) – namely drill and marchpast. On the days there were paper discussions, there would be marchpast practice until lunchtime and paper discussions after. After the two days of paper discussions, the schedule remained the same except for the paper discussions being replaced with drill practice. The selections of the finalists of the various events on Sports Day was done two weeks before the exams commenced.

The next morning, all the students, accompanied by their teachers, headed straight for Paddington Arena after eating breakfast. All day they toiled in the sun, marching for hours on end in the blazing heat of the scorching sun. It wasn't like December at all – the heat almost made it feel like July! Anyhow, the children were given water breaks at regular intervals and were advised by their P.E. teachers to 'move their toes' if they felt giddy. If one of the children marched a little less enthusiastically, they would be energised by a thousand encouraging screams from their teachers who stood near their respective houses (for the teachers also belonged to houses). While the students found the practices nothing short of barbaric torture, they also loved the lemonade and oranges that they were served after an hour of practice. The last one hour was dedicated to practice for the events such as high jump, long jump, 100-metres race, 200-metres race, shotput and the like. During this time, all those who were not participating in the events either gossiped away or enjoyed a good drink of freshly-squeezed cold lemonade in the blazing heat of the December sun. The practices were, however, occasionally disrupted by a slight passing-by drizzle during which all the students were taken under the shamianas at once.

At 1245 hours, everyone returned to school and had lunch, after which each house went to their respective practice rooms. Each of the houses – *Tranquillity* (blue), *Desire* (green), *Credence* (yellow) and *Jubilance* (red) – were assigned two rooms in the school wherein they could practice for the drill and work on their tent decorations. On Sports Day, the coordinators of each section of the school would judge the tent of each house that was to be decorated by handmade props that adhered to the theme they chose, around which even the drill revolved. The generic theme given to each House Captain was '*Elements of Nature*'. As a result, each house chose individual, more specific themes such as *Avatar: The Last Airbender* or the Indian concept of the *Pancha-Bhutas* and the like. Each house also chose their mascots. For instance, the Tranquillity House chose mascots for each element of nature – Water, Earth, Fire, Air and Space – and gave each mascot a song (or two) wherein he/she is the main character and the others supplement. The other houses followed similar ideas for their drill.

It was a tradition for the houses to show their drills to the other houses for the first time on the day before Sports Day as they would be too busy preparing for their own drill/events on the big day. Therefore, there was dire competition and secrecy between the houses, so as to prevent the others from copying ideas, songs or steps. On the day they had to show each other as well, none of the houses revealed their actual steps. They did it with no energy and hid many formations. Although this helped the houses keep their drills a secret, it killed all the fun and deviated from the main purpose of doing so. The next day was to be a big day for all of school; they were to be brought straight to Paddington by bus at 7:45 AM, and the events were to start at 8:30 AM.

On Sports Day, two experienced sports persons were invited to the Paddington Arena as chief guests, apart from the innumerable parents. All the guests were seated in shamianas on one end of the vast main field, while all the Middle & High Schoolers were seated in shamianas according to their houses. The younger children, however, were seated closer to the parents. The teachers were also given a shamiana close to that of the parents. In the relatively smaller throwball/volleyball court behind the guests' shamiana, there were stalls for parents to buy food & drinks from. Similarly, there was a shamiana near the students' shamianas as well that served them breakfast sandwiches, juices, chips and later (at the end of the day) lunch boxes.

Sports Day was done on a large scale with a flawless sound system and a marchpast of extreme coordination! The ceremony began with the lighting of the lamp wherein all the House Captains and the Sports Captain would briskly jog the periphery of the field with a lit torch in their hand and bring it to the Head of School who would mount the torch to the main stand on the dais along with the chief guests. Following the lighting of the torch was the unfurling of the flag which was done with a solemn 18th century music playing in the background. After the opening march, the students marched back to their shamianas, and the events commenced. It all began with the Early Years' Christmas games and then the Elementary School races. The events then proceeded to the Middle & High School races and even races for enthusiastic parents & alumni that were among the guests.

In the meantime, the mascots wore their costumes and did their make-up & hair. Soon, the drills commenced. The first to perform were the Early Years children and next was Elementary School who danced to a medley of catchy and peppy songs. Next up were the seniors – Middle and High. The order of the performances ran thus: Credence, Jubilance, Tranquillity and lastly, their (Tranquillity's) arch rivals, Desire.

At the end of all the events, the bare remaining students assembled yet again in their marchpast lines (although now almost empty) and awaited the results of the Sports Day. The results, announced by the Head of School Ms Victoria, ran thus:

"200-metres race: Desire House
Tug-of-War: Tranquillity House
Decorations: Credence House
Drill: Tranquillity House

Marchpast: Credence House
Rally: Tranquillity House
800-metres race: Jubilance House

Finally, the prize you've all been eagerly waiting for, the winner of the day, is..........the Tranquillity House!!!!!!!"

On hearing this, the Tranquillity House rejoiced for their victory was after a giant *16 years*! They ran the periphery of the main field, none of them feeling the tiredness they felt when they had running practices on the same vast field. They ran with their heads high and their House Flag fluttering in the capable hands of the House Captain. Once they had finished their victory lap, the Tranquillity House returned to their position where they received an award from Ms Victoria. They were thereafter trapped by the paparazzi! All the parents took pictures of their victorious children. The teachers of the Tranquillity House promised the students of the house that they would bring them a big blue-coloured cake to mark their victory for the first time in over a decade.

Soon after all the pomp, the children reassembled for the closing ceremony and thereafter stood solemnly for the national anthem.

CHAPTER ELEVEN

A STIRRING FIELD TRIP!

In January, when school reopened after the winter holidays, it was almost time for the most-awaited event of the year – field trips! Each grade was being taken to a different, exciting destination for their trip between the 16th and 20th of January. Magnolia & Cypress were accompanied by Mr Bill (the history teacher), Ms Lancy (the English Language teacher and the homeroom teacher of Magnolia) and Ms Deah (the High School & Cypress math teacher and the homeroom teacher of Cypress). The orientation for the parents regarding the trip had already happened in early November, wherein they met with the trip organisers for a briefing on the trip. Within weeks, the children's itinerary was sent out, and everyone was sure hyped for the trip!

On the 13th of January, the last weekday before the field trip, each section was called sequentially to the first floor Audio-Visual Room and was briefed by Ms Victoria and Ms Elizabeth. When it was Magnolia's turn, the pupils scrambled into the AV Room, chattering away loudly. However, the moment they caught sight of Ms Victoria, they silenced almost immediately and took their seats in an orderly fashion instead of fighting for seats like they usually did.

Once everyone was settled, Ms Elizabeth spoke ever so legibly and boldly, "Are you all excited for your trip?!?!" At this, the class screamed "YES!" in unison and began speaking to her together. Ms Elizabeth then raised her hand firmly, at which everyone silenced. "We teachers are certainly excited for you all as well. I believe the itinerary has been sent out to your parents and so have the reporting details. In case you have not yet read it, let me tell you now. Everyone is to report at the airport at 6:30 AM sharp on Monday at Departures Gate 3. Is that clear? *Departures Gate 3*. From there, your chaperones – Mr Bill, Ms Lancy and Ms Deah – will hand your identity cards to you, will assign you your trip buddies and will take your attendance. Thereafter, you shall proceed to the terminal and board your flight at 8 AM. Is that understood by all of you?" At this, the students said, "Yes," in unison.

"Ms Elizabeth," asked Stacy, "are we allowed to bring money on the trip? And, are we allowed to buy food on the plane and at the airport?" Ms Elizabeth replied, "Yes, you all are permitted 2000 bucks – remember, not more than that. Further to your question, you are permitted to buy food on the plane and at the airport; however, it is advised that you bring your breakfast from home, but yes, you can buy food. Oh, and one more thing, please remember to wear your school uniform to the airport. Considering the temperature at your destination, you can wear warmer pants & jackets, but you will have to wear your school shirt. This applies for your return journey as well. Another imperative factor to remember is to please pack warm clothes. As written in the mail that I sent out to your parents, the temperature there is expected to be a maximum of 10 degrees and a minimum of negative 2. Therefore, please pack accordingly so as to prevent you from getting sick and spoiling your trip."

"One more thing, children. Please remember that you all are ambassadors of our school and must hence portray it in the best light possible. In order to do that, your current lackadaisical behaviour is not acceptable. The fact that your class was detained from P.E. class a few months ago is not hidden from me. Therefore, please rectify your behaviour and listen to whatever your teachers tell you. Is that fine by you all?" said Ms Victoria in her sweet, supple voice. The children nodded, smirking as they were definitely guilty of the accusation.

As the session ended and the Magnolians walked out of the room, they were welcomed by the next section, who clapped sarcastically at their exit. The Magnolians, taking this as an opportunity, walked through the 'paparazzi' with their heads high in pride, laughing. They were, after all, going away for an entire week all by themselves!

CHAPTER TWELVE

At the Airport

At 6:30 AM on Monday morning, all of Magnolia and Cypress were promptly at Departures Gate 3 of the airport where they were welcomed by their chaperones, personnel from their trip organiser and Ms Elizabeth & Ms Victoria. Then, Ms Lancy and Ms Deah began to hand out the identity cards to their respective class' children. In the meantime, Mr Bill began calling out the order in which the students were expected to line up until they were seated outside their gate inside the airport. All the students were then given their boarding passes and their tickets.

"Your teachers will assign you your trip buddies once you are inside the airport. Kindly remember to be with them at all times, including when you have to go to the washroom – though not *inside* the washroom, of course. No requests will be taken to change your roommates or your travel buddies, so please cooperate," explained Ms Elizabeth right before the students entered the airport.

One by one, all the students bid farewell to their parents and Ms Elizabeth & Ms Victoria and scanned their boarding passes at the entrance of the airport. "Have a good trip, children!" cried Ms Victoria affectionately as they entered the airport. Once everyone was inside, the teachers assigned each student a trip buddy. The buddies were almost to everyone's liking, with a few exceptions. Margaret and Amber were together; Lewis and Harry were together; Samuel and Oliver were together; Eleanor and Laura were together; Amy and Sophie were together; Alice and Hannah were together; and so on. Everyone handed in their check-in baggage to one of the personnel from the trip organising company, who did a mass check-in for all the students. Meanwhile, the students proceeded towards the screening area. While most children got through the screening without any hiccups, Amber was told to remove her boots (as they were of leather) and her carry-on bag was caught for suspicious devices. However, when she showed the airport security that they were solely a digital camera and an MP3 player, she was permitted to pass.

Once they arrived at their departures gate, Gate 8, everyone settled down with their friends. At this time, Ms Deah asked for everyone's attention and announced, "So children, since you are 37 of you and we are 3 teachers, we have decided to split you into 3 groups, one with each teacher. Margaret, Amber, Oliver, Samuel, Ben, Jamie, Eleanor, Laura, Jacob and Jake are with Mr Bill...." and so she continued to announce the groups. Soon after she was finished, the children proceeded to buy themselves food from the shops at the airport. Most of them purchased coffee, burgers and doughnuts. Many children borrowed money from their friends if they did not have enough to buy what they wanted. Others lent money out of generosity or if they saw that their friends did not have adequate money to buy what they wanted. In return, the borrower was expected to buy their lender something when they had the money to. Although this barter did not cause much problem at present, it definitely did through the course of the trip.

Amidst all of the commotion, Amber and Margaret peacefully sat with their bags beside them and their feet stretched out. Amber bit into her home-made ham sandwiches, while Margaret tore nimbly at a cover which had a box of cooked & flavoured beaten rice. "Really, Margaret? Beaten rice?" asked Amber. "Yes, why not! They are my favourite!" replied Margaret. "So, what are you girls doing," asked Mr Bill, placing his bag beside Margaret. "What are you eating, Margaret?" "Beaten rice," replied Amber, rolling her eyes as Margaret giggled at her. "Ahh, I see. And you, Amber?" "Ham sandwiches," she replied. "Healthy kids," he said, nodding his head as if disappointed at their choices. "Margaret, please will you look after my bag as I buy some coffee?" "Sure, sir," she replied.

Soon, everyone had finished breakfast and boarded their flight.

CHAPTER THIRTEEN

A Smoky Experience

After a one-and-a-half-hour flight, the children stretched as they unbuckled their seatbelts and proceeded outside the aircraft, carrying their carry-on backpacks on their backs. As they stepped out of the aircraft and onto the portable staircase that would lead them to a bus which would ferry them to the airport terminal, the pupils were welcomed by an acute sensation of severe cold that sent shivers down their spines. Soon, as they shared their woes to one another, they discovered that there was smoke coming from their mouths as they spoke due to the cold. They immediately pretended to smoke cigarettes, kindling the infants in them.

Once they had collected their luggage from Belt No. 7, the students, teachers and the trip-organising personnel exited the airport, where they were welcomed by more personnel from the travel agent. From there, everyone proceeded towards a 40-seater coach in which they were to be ferried to their hotel. But first, they had to load their luggage in the 'belly' of the bus. Once they boarded, each child took their seat next to their friends and chattered away excitedly.

"Alright, listen children..." began Ms Deah. "Let me inform you priorly that once at the hotel, all of you would have to collect your luggage which would have already been unloaded and kept ready for you at the entrance of the hotel. Then, we shall all gather in the lobby where I will announce your room numbers and roommates and will give you your room keys. After an hour and a half of rest in your rooms, during which you could probably freshen up, we shall leave for the Resin Fort which is only a short drive away. However, after that, we will be driving directly to a place called 'The Beautiful Hamlet', wherein we will eat traditional local food. Let me tell you right now that the drive to The Beautiful Hamlet is going to be a long one, and I would suggest we use the restroom before leaving for the fort." Just as she finished speaking, they arrived at their hotel.

The hotel was located in a very serene place, much secluded from the busy life of the city. Right opposite the hotel stood a massive hill, on which the Resin Fort stood majestically. Around the hotel were lush green trees that bore flowers of heterogenous colours and marvellous fragrances. The overall vibe of the place was truly enchanting.

The children filed down the coach, collected their respective suitcases and dragged them into the hotel lobby. Once everyone was present, the children made a circle around Ms Deah who was announcing the room numbers and roommates and giving the students their room keys. "Please remember what I told you in the bus and make sure to be wearing warm clothes when you come down in one and a half hours. As soon as I give you your roommates, room numbers and room keys, you may proceed towards your room. And please *do not* fight for the elevator. If you can carry your luggage up to your room, please do so and allow others who cannot to use the elevator. Alright?" "Yes, Miss!" cried the entire grade in unison.

"Alright! So, let me start with the girls. Amy, Laura and Eleanor are in room 401; here are your keys. Sophie, Margaret and Amber are in room 402; here are your keys..." As she continued to speak out the numbers, both parties that were announced first proceeded to collect their bags, complaining about their roommates. "Margaret and I had chosen Amy to be in my room. How did she come in your room!?!" exclaimed Sophie, evidently very frustrated with the compromised arrangement. "Well, as much as I would have liked Amy in our room, at least I will not have to bear with both of you fighting day and night, Sophie!" joked Margaret, trying to lighten the mood. "This is not the time to joke, Margaret! Although you may be correct, actually," chuckled Amy. "Well, we will somehow try figuring this arrangement out," said Eleanor who was also clearly not happy with an outsider intruding while she spoke to her best friend, Laura. "I'm just glad I am in the same room as you, Margaret!" whispered Amber into Margaret's ear. Just as Margaret returned a pleasant smile to her crony, the lift arrived. The six girls scrambled into the lift with their luggage and pressed on '4'. Once they reached, Margaret and Eleanor opened their respective rooms – that were beside one another – while Sophie and Amy bid farewell to each other in the most utterly dramatic manner. "Stop it now, you melodramatic queens!" said Amber as she followed Margaret into their room. "Well...goodbye again!" cried Sophie and Amy in unison before they shut their room doors behind them.

The moment Sophie entered her room, she dropped her bags, and her jaw dropped. "THE ROOM IS SO AMAZING!" she cried. "Look at all this! The bathroom is so luxurious! And the beds are so comfy! And the curtains look so royal! I'm not sleeping on the floor tonight, people!" she exclaimed in a metastable state, jumping onto the bed as if to fan off her excitement which almost made her forget the fact that she had been separated from her friend. "Alright, calm down now, Sophie," said Amber as she opened her suitcase to find her towel. "And don't you both worry. I shall sleep on the floor tonight," said Margaret. "Why? I'm sure there is enough room for all three of us to fit into this bed, isn't there?" asked Amber who was now picking out clothes. "Well, maybe, but it will definitely be more comfortable for you both to sleep on one bed and me on another. I get my own space and you guys get more space!" explained Margaret. "We'll see that at night. I'm going for a bath now, okay? You should probably get ready to go too, Sophie!" said Amber as she walked across the large room towards the bathroom. "I don't plan to bathe today," said Sophie. "I'll take bath tomorrow maybe." At this, Amber stopped at the bathroom door and looked at Margaret in disgust, rolling her eyes. "And Margaret, can you turn on the lights or something? It's too dark in here," said Amber. Margaret looked around the room for light switches. "Well, it seems all the lights are already on. Let us get in some natural light." As Margaret opened the curtains, she was taken aback as she definitely did not expect what she saw. She gave out a little cry. "What is it?" asked Sophie, still lying face down on the soft bed. "You guys have to see this!" exclaimed Margaret. At this, both Amber and Sophie approached Margaret, only to find a very royal-looking sofa. It was by the window and decorated with regal, traditional, laced pillows. "This is a perfect place to read!" exclaimed Sophie. "And to take in the sight. Look at the view!" exclaimed Margaret. "Well, now we certainly did not expect *this*, did we!" said Amber, now returning to the bathroom. "Anyways, I shall enjoy this after I bathe. Bye-bye!" Sophie instantly jumped onto the sofa and laid down there with her hands on her head. Margaret chuckled.

Just then, the doorbell rang. "Can you get it?" asked Sophie, almost ordering Margaret. "Yes, sure," she replied, striding across the wooden-floored room. It was Mr Bill and Ms Deah. "Hey girls. Since you are just 3 people, can we remove one of the mattresses that we had laid for you to sleep on the floor? There are two mattresses and you are just three of you," said Ms Deah. "Sure, Miss," said Margaret politely. As Mr Bill and Ms Deah entered the room to remove the extra mattress, they found Sophie lazing on the bed like royalty. They soon exited the room with the extra mattress in their hand, laughing at Sophie's aristocratic behaviour.

Just as Margaret approached the door to close it, Amy appeared. "Hey!" she cried. Startled, Margaret exclaimed, "You just spawned from nowhere!" "Well, too bad. Now, is it alright if we borrow Sophie for a bit?" "Sure," replied Margaret. "Bye!" said Sophie as she scurried off to join her friend whom she much dearly missed. "Don't forget to come back soon! You have to change into warmer clothes before we leave!" cried Margaret as she shut the door. She walked across the room and made herself comfortable on the sofa. She looked out the window and awed at the spectacular, picture-perfect scenery.

"Where is Sophie?" asked Amber, who was already at the bed, folding her clothes. When she saw that Margaret was not listening, she threw a pillow at her, startling her.

"Which world were you lost in?" she laughed. Margaret replied, "The serene beauty of nature is just so truly enchanting. When I look out the window, I forget all the things that are happening here. I forget that I am far away from home and from my parents; I forget that I am sitting on a luxurious sofa in a five-star hotel; the commotion of our classmates chattering loudly outside on the corridor is silenced. It is almost like I am transported to another utopic world where there is peace, love and serenity all around." "You know, the way you are talking is sort of scaring me. It sounds like you are speaking in trans. However, I would not expect anything less from Margaret. Anyway, answer me: where is Sophie?" "Oh, right. She has gone somewhere with Amy," replied Margaret as she got off the sofa, coming back to her senses. "Knowing Sophie, I do not think she will realise that she has to change her clothes before she leaves. She is literally wearing leggings and a tank top in 10 degrees!" exclaimed Amber. "Yes, I know. Which is why I told her to come back in time, so she can change. At worst, we can just ask Eleanor or Laura where Amy and Sophie are," said Margaret as she got out her coat.

At that very moment, the knob of the locked wooden room door turned. A moment later, the bell sounded. "Coming!" cried Margaret as she walked towards the door, only to find Sophie. "Wow! Think of the angel and hear the flapping of her wings!" exclaimed Margaret as she closed the door behind Sophie. Gauging Sophie's behaviour, Margaret and Amber thought something was wrong. They shared glances, and then, Amber spoke out their thoughts, "All okay, Sophie?" "Well, I am in a big dilemma! I need your help! It is very serious!" cried Sophie to her roommates. Further confused, Margaret asked, "What dilemma?" "WHAT DO I WEAR?!?!?!?" "Really?" said

Amber, rolling her eyes. "I realised I packed too cold for the weather! I'll just wear a thick jacket over this shirt, I guess," said Sophie, contemplating. "I sincerely hope you realise that you are wearing a crop top, Sophie, and that it is less than 10 degrees outside," explained Margaret. "Exactly! Here, Margaret and I are wearing stockings under our pants to keep us warm, and you are wearing a crop top?!?! We cannot spend our night looking after you if you get sick, Sophie!" cried a frustrated Amber. "Well, I'll be alright," replied Sophie, drawing a jacket over her. "Wow! Is that what you call thick, Sophie?!? I always thought thick meant wool!" cried Amber. "Calm down, Amber…" said Margaret calmly, thoroughly amused at the happenings in her room and trying hard to push back her laughter.

Suddenly, the girls heard a loud commotion outside their room. Margaret opened the door to see what was happening. She saw that the other students and the teachers were already ready and leaving for the coach. "Quick, guys! Get ready! The others are leaving," said Margaret, shutting the door behind her. Just as she was halfway across the room, the doorbell rang. Margaret swiftly grabbed her backpack and ID card before dashing back to the door to open it. "Come on quick, guys! We are leaving. And do not forget to bring the key downstairs!" cried Mr Bill as he ran down the corridor with the others. "You heard that, come on!" Margaret wore her shoes and stood outside their room, awaiting her buddy. "Hold on! I'm coming too!" cried Amber as she too ran outside the room. "Sophie, please bring the keycard when you are coming!" cried Amber as Margaret dragged her by the arm down the winding old-style staircase that was barely lit, just like the rooms.

CHAPTER FOURTEEN

THE RESIN FORT

In the lobby, Ms Deah was collecting everyone's room keys. Just then, Sophie came running down the stairs and handed in their room keys.

"Alright, everyone! As I said before, we are now headed to the Resin Fort. For those who did not know, that fort over there is where we are going," said Ms Deah, pointing towards the majestic fort that was mounted on the opposite hill. "Now, this is what we are going to do." As Ms Deah continued explaining the itinerary for the rest of the day, a group of boys – including Jamie, Ben, Samuel and some others – were not paying attention and were instead wrestling each other. In the process, one of them knocked over a brass oil lamp that was almost as tall as the children. The sounding THUD and the spillage of oil caught everyone's attention. "Boys!" screamed Ms Lancy. "I thought we had made ourselves explicitly clear that this lackadaisical behaviour is unacceptable! We are not in school! Besides, you all aren't babies anymore! You are *so* lucky that the lamp was not lit, else you would have been badly hurt and could have caused great damage to the hotel as well!" There went another lecture from the teachers, and even the hotel staff, regarding the Magnolians' unacceptable behaviour. In the meantime, the students of Cypress listened quietly, chuckling at their friends-yet-rivals getting scolded at.

Once all the drama had ended, everyone boarded their Volvo sleeper coach. Within minutes, they had reached the Resin Fort. It was truly breathtaking, looking at the ancient stone architecture! The fort was fortified with a moat and a long, high stone wall with majestic bastions.

As beautiful as the surroundings were, the children certainly had a tough time climbing up all the numerous steep stairways in the scorching sun before they reached the entrance to the main fort.

"Hello everyone! I am Sebastian, and I shall be your guide around the Resin Fort. This fort once belonged to King Ethan, whom you may have heard of if you have watched the movie called 'Kingdom of Resin'. The structure that you can see behind me is the main fort, where the royals lived a truly luxurious life. The fort walls that you climbed up to reach here were used for garrisons, who were at the bastions." The children were truly amused by the rich history the place held. "If you may have noticed, there is a huge ramp on the other side of the hill to the side you climbed. That ramp was used to get onto the fort on animals, mostly elephants. The elephants of the area were richly decorated and so were the many forts & palaces, like all the other traditional places in the locality."

"Now, do you see that structure over there?" asked Mr Sebastian, pointing to a structure on his right. Everyone's eyes followed Mr Sebastian's finger, where they found an elevated structure with numerous stone pillars and intricate carvings. "That is the 'Dance Hall'. In the ancient times, during festivities and functions, all the royals and important dignitaries would sit around that hall – where we are standing right now – and watch damsels dance to live music. This was also considered as an olden form of entertainment. Let's go inside now. Come on!" Before heading into the main fort building, a group picture was taken of everyone sitting at the stairs of the Dance Hall. Ms Deah immediately sent it to the parents.

The children filed into the entrance of the fort building. The entrance was a dome shape and had intricate paintings made of natural organic paints, made years ago. The paintings also had traces of a golden colour that were said to be real gold made into a thin foil and pasted onto the ceiling in the gone-by years. Many domes that were arranged in the shape of the letter 'L' led to a vast courtyard.

Once everyone reached the courtyard, Mr Sebastian said, "This is the place where many traditional festivities were celebrated in full pomp. A short distance from this courtyard is a 'Mirror Palace'. At dusk, it is said that the entire palace gets lit up at a particular time, when the sun is at a specific angle. Shall we head there?" "Yes, please!" replied the children, who were eager to see the Mirror Palace despite the scorching heat.

They walked through tunnels and passed many small courtyards, until they reached a courtyard almost as large as the courtyard at the entrance, but much more decorated! The Mirror Palace stood right in front of them, containing mirrors of different shapes and sizes. Opposite the Mirror Palace was the courtyard, decorated with lush green flowering shrubs and a cobbled path running in between, arranging the shrubs in squares. Right at the centre of every alternate square stood a truly regal water fountain, beautifully ornated.

Everyone was mesmerised, lost in awe at the beauty of the area. Mr Bill and Ms Deah captured some candid moments, instantly updating the parents of their progression by sending the photos. Once they were done having fun looking at themselves in the mirrors that aberrated their reflection, the students and teachers left the courtyard and yet again, walking down tunnels and crossing more courtyards, they reached the Ladies' Palace – a two-storeyed palace that was much simpler than the others in the fort.

"In the ancient times, this is the place where the women of the royal family resided. It is believed that while the children and married women lived on the ground floor, the widows lived on the upper floor, secluded from society," explained Mr Sebastian. Following this brief explanation, everyone sat down on the ground, for they were truly exhausted after the long walk in the blazing heat. In the meantime, Margaret and Amber – after sipping on water – approached a wall with engraved writing that described the Ladies' Palace.

"Amber, could you kindly click a photograph on your camera of this plaque and send it to me once you get home?" asked Margaret, who was truly intrigued by the information on the plaque. "Sure!" said Amber, taking out her camera from her backpack. Once Margaret finished reading, the two girls walked back to where their fellow friends and teachers sat. "What were you doing there?" asked Mr Bill. "I was reading that plaque. It is pretty much the story that is narrated in the Kingdom of Resin, with a little more facts and dates," replied Margaret. "Alright, kiddos! Let's leave for the coach. We need to drive all the way to The Beautiful Hamlet!" exclaimed Ms Deah, raising everyone to their feet.

Everyone filed down another set of narrow corridors and vast courtyards, leading to the exit at the other side of the fort. "This, children, was the urn that the Queen of Resin used in the movie, 'Kingdom of Resin', to cook for the love of her life, King Ethan," explained Mr Sebastian, pointing to a large metal urn kept on the side of one of the courtyards enroute.

On the way back to their coach, everyone stopped for a picture downhill with the fort behind them. Suddenly, somebody cried, "Look! That's Comrade Napoleon!" When all the students figured that the child was in fact pointing towards a black boar that was drinking water in the moat, they burst out laughing. "Who is Comrade Napoleon?" asked Ms Deah. "In Literature, we are reading a novel called 'Animal Farm' by George Orwell. In that, Comrade Napoleon parallels to Josef Stalin from the Russian revolution and is a wild boar," explained Margaret. At this, the teachers began laughing as well.

CHAPTER FIFTEEN

THE BEAUTIFUL HAMLET

Once everyone was aboard the bus, the teachers did a quick head count to make sure they had all 37 of their students. Once all the passengers had settled, the bus took off for The Beautiful Hamlet.

The drive from the Resin Fort to The Beautiful Hamlet took a little more than an hour. The journey was from the era of the ancient Resin Kingdom to the new era of machines and technology. While some of the students and Ms Lancy took a nap during the ride, most of the children were singing or listening to music. Soon, the trip-organising personnel agreed to play songs for the children. Despite all the commotion, Ms Lancy slept peacefully, exhausted taking care of the boisterous children, while Amber and Margaret put on an earphone each, connected to Amber's MP3 player, and took in the scenery as they listened to an hour-long piece of truly rejuvenating music.

By dusk, the bus had entered the parking area of The Beautiful Hamlet. As the students and teachers filed down the bus, each was greeted by an acute chill that sent shivers down their spine, forcing them to pull down their woollen caps and zip up their jackets.

The children proceeded into The Beautiful Hamlet, their hands in their pockets throughout, where they were greeted by live local music and men dressed in traditional attire. Once they had entered the main gate of The Beautiful Hamlet, the students were permitted to use the restroom – for it was truly a long drive – before they were split into the three groups that were formed at the airport.

The Beautiful Hamlet simulated how a traditional local village would be, with folk dances, local magic tricks and hutments. Each group of children, led by Ms Lancy, Ms Deah and Mr Bill respectively, was taken to different stations in The Beautiful Hamlet to enable the experiencing of local traditions.

Mr Bill took his group of students to the dance station first, where local ladies danced with a pile of clay pots mounted on their heads. They also encouraged visitors to join them in their dance, minus the clay pots. Mr Bill took a video of students like Margaret and Oliver who were called by the ladies to dance with them.

Next, Mr Bill took his students to the puppet show station. Unfortunately, the next puppet man said that his next show was to happen after half an hour. Hence, Mr Bill decided to bring his students back after they had finished exploring the many other stations. Then, they proceeded towards the magic station.

Each station was surrounded by cots made of woven coir and lined with traditional pillows that were each capable of seating up to six people. The magic station, however, was different. The local magician sat on a raised platform that was shaped like a coiling snake and shaded by a giant plastic snake head. The platform was faced by a semicircle of red steps on which the audience could sit. The ambience created mystic vibes.

As Mr Bill and the children took their seats among the many other viewers, the magician commenced his show by uttering a bunch of ridiculous-sounding words that made the audience laugh. "Shhh!!!!" cried the magician, silencing his intrigued audience instantaneously. The magician brought out a woven basket from behind him, covered by a cloth. Thereafter, he stretched his hands over the basket. He moved his hands above the basket in circles, murmuring a little chant to himself. Finally, after a few seconds, he stopped moving his hands and looked up at his audience who were watching intently. He smiled. He then looked at the basket. Suddenly, something began to move in the basket! "I reckon that's a snake!" cried Mr Bill, trying to scare his students. He stretched his hand in front of them and said, "Stay back." The magician picked up the basket and showed it to the audience, holding onto the cloth. The anxious students stared at the basket intently, trying to catch a glimpse of the moving creature inside it. Finally, when the magician pulled out the cloth in an ever so dramatic manner, they were delighted to see a white dove flutter out of the basket and land on the magician's shoulders. He then wrapped the dove in the cloth that he had priorly used to cover the basket, restraining the bird. The next moment, when he unwrapped the cloth, all that was left in the cloth was a piece of newspaper.

"You! Come!" cried the magician, pointing at Mr Bill. Surprised and delighted at the same time, Mr Bill, who was recording the entire magic show, handed his phone to Margaret who was sitting beside him. "Record me, please," he said to her. While Mr Bill climbed onto the elevated snake-shaped platform, his students cheered him on, "Whoo-hoo, Mr Bill! Go sir!" "Look me," said the magician.

Obeying his words, Mr Bill looked at the magician. "Hold 'zis coin." Mr Bill took the coin that the magician offered him. "Now, but 'zat in you bocket," said the magician. Mr Bill put the coin into his pocket. Thereafter, the magician performed a similar procedure as he did to the basket, murmuring a little chant as he moved his hands mystically around Mr Bill's pocket. As Mr Bill and his students laughed, the magician instructed, "Bull you bocket inside-out." When Mr Bill did so, he found that the coin was missing! "Now, ztand ztill," ordered the magician sternly. The magician got up and walked towards the other end of the platform. When Mr Bill turned around to see what the magician was doing, the magician snapped, "I zay ztand ztill!" The audience chuckled. The magician then approached Mr Bill with a steel bucket in his hand. "Al-ana yushahidu," said the magician in his language. Thereafter, the magician commenced his trick. He cupped Mr Bill's palm and brought the bucket below it. Coins dropped! He then told Mr Bill to open his mouth. When the magician brought the bucket close to Mr Bill's mouth, coins fell out from there too! He continued this until the bucket was filled with coins. Mr Bill was then sent back to his seat. Thereafter, the magician brought out a bagpiper. Pointing it to another cloth-covered basket, he began to play it. As he played, the cloth began to wrinkle up into the shape of a snake that danced to the magician's tunes. The audience was truly amused! Once the magician ended his tricks, the audience filed out of a tiny gate that was bolted to the sides of a gap formed between the red steps. As Mr Bill and his students walked out, Ms Lancy arrived with her students, ready to watch the magician's next show.

After exploring a few more stalls, Mr Bill took his students around a bonfire to warm them up a little before taking them to eat a traditional feast. As they waited for the others around the bonfire, Jamie and Jake requested Mr Bill if they could check out the gaming stalls. At his approval, they proceeded.

"Welcome, kiddos!" said one of the stall keepers. The boys smiled. "What game you like to try out? How about bowling alley, eh?" asked the man. "Well, sure! Why not!" replied Jake. The man took the boys to the bowling stall where Jamie and Jake were able to knock down five of the eight pins and six of the eight pins respectively. "'Zat would be phiphty bucks, kid," said the man once they were done playing. "Now, you want to zry archery?" asked the man, sweetly. "Sure!" said Jamie. "Would that be fifty as well?" "Yes," said the man politely. The boys then went ahead to the archery stall where both of them won a prize each for striking the target. "Now, you like to zry 'zis stall, kid?" asked the man, now rather imposingly. With no other choice, for the man was being very imposing, the boys agreed. Soon, the boys had already spent 500 bucks each, when Mr Bill called them over for dinner. "Phew!" exclaimed the boys in unison as they ran towards their peers.

The children filed behind their respective group teachers towards the dining area. Here, they were to take off their shoes (and preferably socks, for the ground was too muddy), wash their legs at a tap and thereafter proceed towards the seating area. The seats were simply cushions on the floor while the tables were made of wood and at a perfect height for the seated visitors to eat from. The seating area was divided into many sections, out of which two of the sections were used by the students and teachers. Each section, which was essentially a large rectangular room with a thatched roof and walls that were as tall as an average Asian's hips, had two rows of tables and cushions (seats) that faced each other, lined along the longer sides of the room. Thus, the students from both rooms were able to talk to one another from over the wall.

The serving procedure was lengthy, in adherence to the local traditions. The servers first arrived with a jug in their glove-clad hands, from which they poured warm water on everyone's hands to cleanse them before eating. Next, the servers arrived with plates made of woven palm leaves which they placed at the bottom-centre of each table. Following the plates were ten bowls per person, also made from woven palm leaves. Thereafter, a line of men filed into the room, serving a dish each. Each bowl was either filled with a curry, a sweet or curd whereas the plates were filled with breads of different types, colour and texture.

"Wow! This is sure extravagant," cried Margaret, amused at the amount of food she was being served. "I have never seen so much food on one table in my life!" exclaimed Amber, who was seated beside her. "Oy Margaret, do you plan on finishing all of that?" cried Oliver from the seats across, amidst numerous men continually filing in with more food. "Well, definitely not!" cried Margaret back, trying to get her feeble voice across the room. Finally, just as everyone assumed there was no more food left to come, two men arrived with trays filled with pots of butter. A pot was kept for each person. "'Zis iz to eat with 'ze breadz," said one of the men as he served.

Finally, once all the dishes were served, the children commenced eating. "I am going to call my family back home and show them what we are eating," said Mr Bill, who was sitting beside Margaret. Mr Bill smacked his lips as he showed off the scrumptious food to his family, causing them to feel hungry as well. "Now, I am going to call Mr

Richard and make him jealous as well," said Mr Bill as he grinned, dialled and gobbled up his food at the same time. As he spoke to Mr Richard, Margaret said to Amber, "I really do not think I will be able to finish even one of these breads or curries. I am simply going to take a bite or two from each bread and probably just take a lick from each curry for the sake of tasting it, if not finishing it. Besides, I presume I will probably end up finishing nothing on my plate except the curd." "I swear!" cried Amy from across the room. "I'll probably eat more than *you* though, Margaret. You barely eat anything! Even if it is just school food," she joked. "Fair point," said Margaret.

Once everyone was done, they got up from their seats with great difficulty and proceeded to wash their hands. "Oh, I feel like my stomach is going to explode," complained Amber as she washed her hands. "Likewise. All that food is making me hot!" replied Margaret. As everyone was putting on their shoes, Ms Deah announced, "I heard there is a maze somewhere nearby. What say? Shall we go?" "YES!" cried all the children, excited. "Well, at least your food will somewhat get digested and you won't be burping in the bus," joked Mr Bill. "Ew, sir! That's utterly gross!" cried Oliver as Mr Bill chuckled.

Everyone entered the maze in a haste. While most of the children struggled to find their way out, Margaret and Amber could see the exit. As Amber began running towards the exit, Margaret pulled her back and took her through another route. "Why on earth would you do that?" asked Amber. "It's not fun if we directly find our way out! Let's have some fun," replied Margaret as Amber rolled her eyes at her. "You guys! I'll help you! Just follow what I tell you!" cried Eleanor from above with Laura by her side. "How are they there?" asked Amber, amused. "Well, it so happens that they never entered the maze. I remember that there used to be a camel-riding station here many years ago, when I had come as a child. Now, nothing except the wooden staircase that we use to climb onto the camel is left. That is what they are on," explained Margaret. "I see. Can we at least follow their instructions?" asked Amber. "Sure," replied Margaret.

Soon, everyone was out of the maze and in line, ready to board their coach. After a headcount, the teachers led the children towards their bus. As soon as they got in, they felt a nice warmth that they had thoroughly missed, except when around the bonfire.

The ride back to the hotel was rather uneventful. While most children fell asleep, the ones who were awake sat in silence, too filled with food to talk, play or sing.

By 10 PM, the children were back at the hotel.

They filed down the bus sleepily and groggily, sounding 'Brrrrsss' as they got off the bus, for they were yet again welcomed by an extreme chill in the dead of the night.

Once in the lobby, Ms Deah handed over the children's room keys.

CHAPTER SIXTEEN

A 'SLEEPLESS' NIGHT

As Margaret unlocked their room with Amber standing closely behind her, Sophie bid farewell to her dear friend, Amy, who had to return to her 'torture' with Laura and Eleanor. Funny enough, Laura and Eleanor thought the same about Amy.

While Margaret and Amber had already begun changing into their night clothes, Sophie sauntered into the room, flinging her bag onto the bed and placing herself comfortably on the reading nook that they had discovered behind the curtains.

"Brr...it sure is cold in here!" she cried as Margaret made herself comfortable on the wooden table on the side of the room, near the reading nook. "I wouldn't be surprised, considering the temperature outside!" replied Amber, walking towards Margaret and Sophie. "What are you doing?" asked Amber when she saw Margaret engrossed in writing a book. "I am just making a diary entry of the things we did today. That way, I can remember our field trip in the years to come. One day, maybe, if someone finds my diary like they found Anne Frank's, maybe *everyone* will come to know about our field trip and my life!" replied Margaret. "Yes, except Anne Frank actually struggled to live on while you are living in luxury," joked Amber. "Sure, but nobody said you need to have a tragic life to have an interesting biography!" joked Margaret.

In half an hour, "Margaret! Are you done yet?" asked a frustrated Amber. "Almost……yes! Done," replied Margaret, closing her book and keeping it safely inside her suitcase. "Anyone want jaggery pieces?" asked Margaret. "No, thanks," replied Amber, thoroughly disgusted. "It is good for the cold and is rich in iron!" replied Margaret, popping two pieces of jaggery into her mouth before closing a small orange box with a yellow lid that contained the jaggery.

Just then, the doorbell rang. "I'll go get it," said Margaret, walking towards the door. It was Mr Bill and Ms Deah. "You kids better be in bed right now for we have a long day ahead tomorrow. Please make sure to wake up at half past 6 tomorrow, alright?" explained Ms Deah. "Definitely, Ms Deah," replied Margaret in an utmost mature manner. "And try not to hog the bathroom by getting explosive diarrhoea tomorrow morning!" joked Mr Bill as he advanced towards the next room with Ms Deah. "Ew. Does he necessarily *have* to make an explosive diarrhoea joke at least once *every* day?" asked a disgusted Sophie as Margaret closed the door. "Come on – let us all get to bed. As Ms Deah said, we have a long day tomorrow! We have to drive towards our next destination. I believe it is a four-hour drive by coach," said Margaret, making her bed ready. Margaret, as had priorly announced, was to sleep on the mattress that was laid on the floor.

Without further procrastination, Margaret turned off the lights, laid her bedsheet and pulled her blanket over her. She then set her alarm for half past 5 in order to get ready leisurely before her roommates awoke. Likewise, Amber and Sophie jumped into their soft, bouncy bed. Sophie tugged at the blanket, pulling it towards herself. Angry, Amber decided to have some fun.

"Hi. My name is Suzie," she said, in the voice of a creepy infant doll. "WHAT WAS THAT?" asked Sophie with her ears pricked up, her forehead wrinkled and her eyes wide open. "That was just Amber, Sophie. Who else could it be, making such ludicrous sounds?" replied Margaret groggily, turning over. "What on earth is ludicrous?" asked Sophie. She got up. She peered over Amber and down at Margaret, who was already fast asleep. "You know, Margaret sort of looks like Queen Elizabeth getting a wasp treatment," concluded Sophie. "What on earth is a wasp treatment?" asked Amber, curious. "I saw this video on YouTube that showed Queen Elizabeth lying down in a similar way to Margaret right now and wasps stinging her face. Apparently, it makes you look young," explained Sophie, returning to her prior horizontal position. "Now, that sounds painful," said Amber. "Anyways, forget about Queen Elizabeth! Let me tell you something interesting," said Amber. "Yes?" said Sophie, intrigued. "At night, I get these sights of peculiar-looking ladies walking around my room. For instance, right now, I see Suzie. I see the hazy image of a pale lady clad in black, with skin as white as snow and lips as red as blood. Her hair is black as well and has been left open. It is so silky that even a slight breath could make it fly as if there was a storm. She has hazel eyes, glowing brightly in the dark and shaped like that of a cat..." As Amber continued to describe in a solemn voice the imaginary lady that she claimed to be able to see, Sophie screamed, "AAAAAAAAAAAAAAAA!!!!!!! STOP THIS INSTANT, AMBER! YOU ARE FREAKING ME OUT!"

"Well, the funny part is, back in the day, whenever I have tried to touch these ladies, I either walk right through them or they disappear into a puff of smoke," continued Amber. "Margaret! Please help! Your dear friend Amber is freaking me out really bad!" pleaded Sophie to Margaret, who did not respond. "Margaret?" asked Sophie. She got up yet again. Amber turned too. They peered down at Margaret. She did not move an inch. "Margaret?" called Sophie yet again, her voice cracking in fear. "Maybe Suzie possessed Margaret!" joked Amber. "Shut up," said Sophie.

"Do you think she is dead?" asked Amber. "I think so," replied Sophie. The next moment, Amber picked up a pillow and threw it at Margaret. When she still did not wake up, "I really do think she is dead," said Amber. "Come – let us check," said Sophie, pulling Amber out of the bed. They tiptoed towards Margaret cautiously in the dark. Thereafter, they together shook Margaret violently, finally ruining her sleep. "What is it?" asked Margaret groggily, rubbing her eyes. "We thought you were dead!" declared the two girls in unison. "Huh? What do you mean?" asked Margaret, half asleep. "Basically, you did not react to what we told you or to the pillow that we threw at you. That is why we thought you died," explained Amber. "Obviously! How do you expect a person who is sleeping to respond to your silly questions?" replied Margaret. "Now get back to sleep, you two. Did Ms Deah not tell us that we have a long day tomorrow and that we have to wake up early?" "Yes, but Amber is scaring me!" complained Sophie. "She claims to be able to see random ladies at night and is even describing some lady called Suzie whom she claims to see right now!"

While Sophie was busy explaining the happenings that Margaret had missed, Amber creeped towards Sophie silently. She suddenly placed her hand on Sophie's shoulder. "AAAAA!!!!! What was that?!?!" screamed a horrified Sophie. "That was just Amber. Calm down, Sophie," said Margaret, annoyed. "Now stop annoying me and get back to sleep." "Can you please come and sleep on the bed with us? Amber is scaring me a lot!" pleaded Sophie to Margaret. "Of course not! Can you not see that I was already sleeping?" replied Margaret. "Please, Margaret!" cried Sophie. "No! Not in a million years! Now go back to sleep, you two! Or at least please do not disturb me!" replied Margaret, pulling her blanket over her and turning over. "Will you wake us up tomorrow?" asked Amber. "Sure," replied Margaret as she returned to her slumber.

"There she goes," said Amber, laughing as she got back into bed with Sophie. Amber continued to scare Sophie. Eventually, however, Sophie began to laugh it off, trying to hide her fear. Once Amber realised that Sophie was not getting scared anymore, she too fell asleep.

Sophie, however, was awake until late in the night. She was thoroughly frightened by the description of Suzie and hence could not get sleep. Therefore, she continually looked around to make sure nobody came in her proximity. Eventually, though, she too fell asleep.

CHAPTER SEVENTEEN

THE LONG DRIVE

At 6 AM, Margaret awoke with a start. She looked at her alarm clock beside her, only to realise that she had slept through the alarm. "Oh no! And here I was, trying to wake up early so that I could get ready before the others," said Margaret, neatly folding her blanket.

She rolled up the mattress she was provided with. She then removed the batteries from her alarm clock and put them into a case, along with the clock, which she then placed into her bag. She took out her toothbrush and paste and dashed into the restroom, turning on the lights near the entrance to the room, which was also near the entrance to the restroom. Within minutes, she was out again to grab herself some clothes – which she had already kept ready the previous night – and her soap. She dashed into the bathroom yet again and finished bathing in less than five minutes. Thereafter, she came out of the bathroom to apply moisturiser on her face.

Right then, the doorbell rang. She opened the door, just to find Mr Bill. "Good morning, Margaret. I see you are ready already," he said. "Please do wake up your friends as well because it is already quarter to seven. Please be downstairs for breakfast by 7 AM. You can return to your rooms after breakfast to collect your bags and to use the restroom if you wish." "Thank you, Mr Bill," replied Margaret. She then closed the door and walked towards the bed where Amber and Sophie lay sleeping peacefully and occasionally snoring. "Guys, wake up! It is already 6:45 and we have to be downstairs by 7 o'clock! Wake up, quick!" she cried. When they did not listen, Margaret first approached Amber and shook her by the arm. She finally woke up and groggily walked towards the washroom. Once she was in the washroom, Margaret called out to Sophie. Eventually, she too awoke. As Amber changed her clothes and Sophie used the restroom, Margaret folded their bedsheets and completed her final last-minute packing of possessions such as her glass case. Thereafter, she opened a pocket in her bag, took out her identity card and put it around her neck. Finally, the girls proceeded for breakfast, each wearing a jacket and their respective identity cards. Although they were relatively late, they were one of the first students to arrive for breakfast.

After a scrumptious and filling breakfast, the children scurried up to their rooms to collect their luggage and scurried back down with them. As the luggage was being loaded into the 'belly' of the coach, the children enjoyed their last moments in the hotel, adoring the view of the Resin Fort on the mountain across. Soon, once all the luggage was loaded, the teachers led the students into the bus before doing a final headcount. Once the presence of all 37 students and 3 teachers was confirmed, the bus set off on a four-hour drive towards their next destination, which so happened to be a national tiger park.

The drive started off wonderfully, with all students filled with excitement. While the back of the bus was teeming with children chattering and singing, the front was relatively quieter. This was due to the sole reason that many were engrossed in watching anime on Mr Bill's phone, which he held up for everyone to watch. In the meantime, Amber, who had grabbed the window seat, took out her MP3 player and plugged in her earphones. As she did so, Margaret, who was seated beside her, watched her in a rather peculiar fashion. "What?" asked Amber, pausing her music as she looked at Margaret. "I thought this field trip was to spend time *together*, not alone by listening to songs while everyone around you is talking and having fun," replied Margaret, annoyed. "I do not see what else I can do on a four-hour drive, Margaret," defended Amber. "You did this even on our drive from The Beautiful Hamlet. Do you remember?" said Margaret, with frustration seeping in her voice as she spoke. "Yes. I also remember that you slept while I did so," replied Amber. "So do you expect me to sleep through the drive?" asked Margaret. "No. That's not what I meant. What I meant is you can figure out something to do as I listen to songs," replied Amber, resuming her music. A moment later, Margaret nudged Amber. Taking off her earphones, Amber looked at Margaret. "Can I at least sit by the window please?" asked Margaret. "Fine, I guess. It's the least I can do," replied Amber as she moved her backpack and herself onto the seat on the aisle. "Thank you," replied Margaret, now pleased. She enjoyed the rest of the drive by looking out the window.

"Hey Margaret! What are you doing looking out the window for hours?" asked Amy from behind. "Amber refuses to not listen to music, and hence, I am taking in the view," replied Margaret. "Ah, I see. Now that's sad. Would you like to speak with us?" offered Amy politely. "Thanks, but I think I shall stick to looking out the window into the scenery," replied Margaret softly.

Approximately four hours into their drive, the bus stopped by a café. Everyone got off, only to be greeted by the blazing sun. The café had a relatively clean restroom which was accessible through a souvenir store. "I suggest you kids wait until we go to the market where local craftsmen sell their products. Personally, I believe the products in this store are a little overpriced," advised Mr Bill. "Yes, I think so as well," said Margaret to Amber, Amy, Sophie and Stacy. "Have you seen the cost of a Kit-Kat? It costs a hundred bucks! Back home, it costs less than fifty," said Stacy as the others nodded in agreement.

"I think you guys should just use the washroom here and go back to the bus," said Ms Deah. "We do not have much time to waste." Hence, the children proceeded towards the restrooms as the teachers proceeded to grab a cup of tea. Within minutes, the children were readily seated in the bus, only to find that their teachers were missing. "Where are our teachers?" asked Sophie. "Look there! They are drinking tea!" exclaimed Jamie, pointing towards the café.

Soon, they too returned. In another hour, they arrived at their hotel.

CHAPTER EIGHTEEN

THE ART WORKSHOP

"Welcome to the National Park Resort, children!" exclaimed the manager of the hotel at the sight of the children filing down the bus with their luggage. The resort opened onto a vast grassy ground and a cobbled path beside it for vehicles and/or walking. The rectangular ground was surrounded by walls of shrubs from all sides except one of the longer ends, which opened onto the cobbled path and the hotel buildings. This end was, however, lined with relatively short trees. The edge of the ground near the entrance gate had a small park for children with rustic swings, slides and merry-go-rounds. Behind the ground was a large swimming pool that lay on a slightly raised platform. Reclined beach chairs and umbrellas surrounded the pool. The rooms were in the main building, and the reception was in another cottage-like structure beside the main building. The main building faced both the ground and the pool with an intricately designed façade which made it resemble that of the Resin Fort.

"Let me tell you all some things before you head to your rooms," explained the manager. "Firstly, please do not enter the swimming pool or its surroundings; this is solely for your safety. Secondly, we request you to kindly keep in mind that the resort hosts other guests as well, and hence, some decorum is required. Thirdly, it is requested that you restrict your movement around the resort to solely the first floor, where your rooms will be, and this ground. Fourthly, all meals will be served in that hall downstairs," At this, he pointed towards a flight of descending stairs. Near this was also a small souvenir store. "Now, you may first freshen up in your respective rooms and thereafter come downstairs for lunch. I presume you all must be starving!" Ms Deah immediately began distributing the room keys. Unlike normal hotel room keys, which are cards, the room keys of this resort were actual keys. The room was to be unlocked using the key, and the power to the room would turn on when the keychain – a large brass key – was inserted in the provision. The roommates were to remain the same, disappointing Sophie and Amy. Once all the children had finished their lunch, they were allowed some time to rest in their rooms, before their activities in the evening. During this time, most of the students either loitered around the corridors or hung out in others' rooms.

In the evening, all the students were called downstairs to the ground for some fun activities and a workshop before they watched a movie on the park's most famous tiger. While the teachers made themselves comfortable on chairs, the students were made to stand in a circle by the head organising personnel, named Andy, who was also the person accompanying the children for the entirety of their trip (from and back to the airport).

"Hello children, my name is Andy. Now, before we start our main activities, let me boot up your energy. Are you ready?" he exclaimed. When the children replied in disinterest, he asked louder, "I cannot hear you! Are you all ready?" At this, the children forcefully screamed, "YES!!!!" "Alright! Let us start then! From when I say 'start' to when I stay 'stop', you all have to repeat all that I say and all that I do. Is that understood?" he asked. When the children nodded, he announced, "START!"

First, Andy made the children wave their hands up in the air, touch their knees, spin around and the like. Next came the fun part. Andy jumped with his hands in the air, squatted down to the ground, turned around while clapping his hands and finally moved his hips in a circular fashion while squatting, saying "JACUZZA!" At this, the children burst out laughing and many hesitated to repeat this sequence of actions. However, although reluctantly, everyone repeated what Andy did, laughing their hearts out. Thus, Andy made the children repeat the entire process up to 5 times, before moving on to the next game.

"The teachers are free to join this game as well, if they wish to. In this game, all of us are going to successively count from 1 onwards sequentially. However, there is a catch. If the number contains the digit 4, you must clap once; if the number contains the digit 7, you must turn around twice while scratching your chin. Those who fail to follow these are out. However, the game begins with one, and not the number that the ousted person stopped at. Is that fine? I trust there is no confusion," explained Andy. "Sir, I have a question. What if the number is 47 or 74. What do we do then?" asked Daniel. "Then, you must do both!" exclaimed Andy. Intrigued by the game, Mr Bill came rushing and took his place between Alice and Margaret. This game was thoroughly enjoyed by all, even Ms Lancy and Ms Deah who were seated, and almost ousted everyone from the game. The last standing winner was

Alice. "Congrats, Alice! Well played!" said Mr Bill, shaking Alice's hand and hugging her as she replied, "Thank you, sir."

"Next up is the passing-the-balloon-and-running game. All of you are going to be split into three groups, two groups having 12 people and the third having 13. Each group will be positioned in one single line, each member standing one behind the other. I will give each group a balloon which you have to pass to the person behind you from between your legs. The last person in the line has to run to the front of the line, carrying the balloon, and continue the game. Whichever team has all its members run to the front once wins the game. Do you all like the game?" "YES!" replied the children, excited and nervous. When the game commenced, the children screamed excitedly as Mr Bill cheered them on while capturing it on video.

Later in the evening, the children were seated on the ground for an art workshop. The workshop was conducted by personnel from the National Park Art Academy, who would be teaching the children how to paint the eyes of a tiger. "Children, we have decided that whoever makes the best artwork would be awarded. The judges for the competition will be these honourable personnel from the National Park Art Academy," announced Andy.

As soon as the demonstration was over, the children got to work. While Ms Deah and Ms Lancy too were engrossed in making their own artwork, Mr Bill had called Mr Richard on a video call and was showing him the happenings at the resort. Each child had created a masterpiece thereby putting the judges in a dilemma. Finally, once everyone had submitted their artwork, the judges got to work as the children proceeded to watch a movie on the National Park's most famous tiger, which had eventually become the world's most famous tiger – Samaka.

"Samaka, born in the spring of 1997, was the National Park's most majestic huntress," spoke the narrator of the documentary they watched. "Unlike usual tigresses, Samaka bore five litters over a period of seven years – from 1999 to 2006. Out of her eleven cubs, she had four males and seven females. Her name resonated worldwide after she displayed tremendous strength and valour by defeating a 14-foot mugger crocodile. One of her bolder offspring from her third litter, Jamila, defeated her mother and took over not only the entire National Park, but also the National Park Fort – Samaka's prior abode.

Thereafter, Samaka shared space along with one of her mates – Dhukir. Soon, however, Dhukir died as a result of a fatal wound incurred while hunting. Samaka was thus left alone yet again. Over time, Samaka began to grow weaker due to starvation.

Meanwhile, Jamila attracted male tigers and had given birth to three rearing cubs. However, some time in 2013, Jamila disappeared out of the blue. Since her body hasn't yet been discovered, she is considered dead. However, this left the fort open for anyone to conquer. Thus, Samaka returned to her abode.

For a brief period of time, she was healthy. However, after getting defeated by one of her male cubs, she was once found gasping for breath, leading to her death in 2016. Thereafter, one of her other cubs from her third litter, Muhlima, took over her mother's territory.

Samaka was given a respectful funeral by the Government Wildlife Wing and continues to be considered the 'World's Most Famous Tiger', after the documentary made on her."

After this educating yet touching story of Samaka, the tigress, Andy arrived with the artwork. "The winner, as selected by the experienced artists from the National Park Art Academy, is Margaret Scott," saying this, he returned Margaret's artwork to her. "Margaret, please do remind me to get you a gift at the airport before you depart on your return journey," said Andy as he returned the rest of the artworks. Margaret was overjoyed! "How could I have probably made the best art?" asked Margaret to her friends, gazing at her work in amazement.

After the movie, the children headed down the staircase that led to the dining hall. They were greeted by hot, scrumptious food which they gulped down within minutes before retiring for the night. After all, they needed the rest before going on an early-morning game drive! However, Magnolians being Magnolians, nobody fell asleep early that night!

CHAPTER NINETEEN

An Early-Morning Game Drive

This time with success, Margaret awoke at 5 AM, an hour before the expected time. Yet again, just as she got ready, Mr Bill rang the doorbell as a wake-up call. "Margaret! I know you are awake! Please wake up the others as well!" he cried.

"Amber, Sophie, wake up! It is 6 o'clock. We have to go down for milk and cookies at half past 6," called Margaret, putting her alarm clock into her bag. Seeing that neither of them had budged, she yanked their blankets off them. "Margaret!" they snapped in frustration. While Margaret forcefully pulled Amber out of the bed, Sophie pulled up the blanket yet again. When Amber was out of the washroom and fishing for a change of clothes in her bag, Margaret woke up Sophie as well. As Amber and Sophie took their time to get dressed, Margaret folded her roommates' blankets, put away her belongings and put her identity card around her neck. Before she hung her backpack over her shoulders, she took her much insulating jacket and gloves in her hands. She then proceeded towards the door and told Amber and Sophie as she clutched the door handle, "Guys, I am going to wait for you outside for ten minutes. If you do not come by then, please lock the door and come down yourselves as I am going to have my milk." Saying this, she walked out the door and slammed the door behind her. "Margaret! Wait up! I am coming too!" screamed Amber, grabbing her identity card and backpack as she raced towards the door to open it. "Sophie, please do not forget to lock the door and bring the keys!" reminded Amber as she shut the door behind her.

Amber and Margaret trotted down the stairs and out of the main hotel building. They then headed towards the descending staircase that led to the restaurant. There, they were greeted by their teachers and with cookies and milk. While few of the children took milk, most of them took tea. As they gulped down their milk and cookies, Ms Deah stood up to announce, "Children! May I have your attention please?" At this, the children quietened. "Thank you. Now, listen to me carefully. You shall not wander off into any canter you wish to. I will let you know which canter you will be in. For now, let us name them as Canter 1 and Canter 2. Ms Lancy, Mr Bill and Andy will accompany the students aboard Canter 1, while I will accompany those aboard Canter 2. Over to Andy, who will brief you about the rules of the National Park."

"Thank you, Ms Deah. I hope you guys enjoyed your milk and cookies. Now, I would like to brief you about some rules that need to be followed when seated in the canter and when in the National Park. Firstly, let me remind you that you are going into the wild in open canters. By that, I mean that the canters do not have a roof and that the border between you and the Park is simply a metal door and a grill. Therefore, *please* do not stick your hand out of the canter. Secondly, feeding any animal within the premises of the Park, be it birds or monkeys, is strictly forbidden. Hence, kindly refrain from doing so. Thirdly, if you wish to see any animals, silence is imperative. As you may know, loud sounds – such as loud talking, laughter or screams – can scare away animals, especially tigers. Thus, by doing so, you will be lowering the probability of spotting a tiger. Lastly, it goes without saying that you must follow your teachers' instructions at all times. I trust you will abide by these rules. Just to make it clear, these are not meant to restrict you from having fun; in fact, it is to make you enjoy *more* and keep you safe at the same time. Alright?" explained Andy.

Thereafter, Ms Deah announced who would be in which canter, making the children stand in two lines. Once they and their canters were ready, the children filed up the staircase and took their seats in their respective canters. In Canter 2, the children took their seats thus: Lewis and Margaret, Eleanor and Laura, Sophie and Amy, Adam and Holly, Jake and Luke, and the rest of the children seated together in the back row. Ms Deah and the guide for Canter 2 took their seats right at the front of the canter, facing the children. "Hey Margaret!" cried Amy from behind the canter. "I'm sure you're happy sitting there, right in front of the teacher," she joked. "Yes, totally!" cried Margaret. "Why is that, may I know?" asked Ms Deah. Lewis replied mockingly, "Miss, she just likes being near teachers. Don't you, Margaret?" "Yes, I do. That is solely because the area around teachers is generally calmer than the back of the bus, where everything is a ruckus," replied Margaret.

Once the headcount was taken in both canters, the engine of the canters revved and began their journey to the National Park. The drive to the park was less than ten minutes. Once there, they were greeted by a board saying, 'WELCOME TO THE NATIONAL PARK'. Inside the gate stood a massive vermillion-coloured building. A board at the entrance of the building stated 'National Wildlife Department'. After the canters were registered at the entrance, they proceeded to the interiors of the park. "The park has been divided into 10 zones. Out of those, we will be exploring zone 3 today as the tour guides on duty yesterday told us that they had spotted a tiger in zone 3," explained the guide onboard Canter 2 to Ms Deah. Margaret listened closely as well.

The drive from the National Wildlife Department building to the entrance of the zones was truly very scenic. For the first part of the journey, there were lush-green trees of a dense forest on both sides of the road. Next, they came across a large rocky hill on one side, with waterfalls trickling down. According to the guide, a tiger was once spotted on the rocky hill. Finally, they reached the road from which the zones branched out.

Although the experience was lovely hitherto, everyone was freezing in the 2-degree frosty forest air. The canters soon came to the entrance of Zone 3, which was an ancient stone structure that was now covered in wild creepers. "This looks similar to the structures of the National Park Fort that we saw in the documentary on Samaka yesterday," said Margaret as she analysed the structure. "Rightly said, child. This used to be one of the fort entrances in the olden days," explained the guide. Margaret smiled as she looked intently at the structure until they drove through it and into the zone. "The currently active tigers in zones 3, 4 and 5 are called Cal, Edith and Esther. In fact, they are a family," explained the guide. "So, if you spot a tiger in any of these zones, you can infer that it may be one of them."

The Park was surprisingly dry. Probably due to the extremely chilly weather, all that remained of trees were their trunks and branches, and shrubs were nothing but a bundle of sticks. Nevertheless, the children spotted innumerable animals! First, they spotted two baby owls perched on the branch of a tree. Next, they spotted many types of deer like the sambar deer and the spotted deer. While enjoying the scenery, the children's teeth chattered due to the cold. "The place is so cold that my hands feel cold even inside these gloves!" complained Lewis. "I suggest you sit on your hands. That way, your body heat will supplement the insulation provided by the gloves in warming your hands," said Margaret, also doing what she advised.

As they drove around the forest, the children's eyes and ears were sharply scanning their surroundings to spot any movement that could possibly be that of a tiger. Meanwhile, Holly opened a packet of biscuits as she was hungry. Just as she was about to put it into her mouth, a bird swooped down and swiftly snatched it away. "Holly! Please put away that packet of biscuits! It is not safe to feed these to the birds," cried Andy from the other canter. Immediately, Holly stuffed her biscuits back into her backpack, horrified by the sight of a flock of birds approaching her. Seeing this, all the children tightly clasped their headgear so as to prevent the birds from flying away with them and being left without any protection in the bitter cold. When the flock flew away, the canters proceeded.

"Stop the canter!" cried Amy, forcing the driver to sharply press on the brakes. "What is it, dear? Are you alright?" asked Ms Deah, her forehead creasing in worry. "Yes, Miss. However, I do not think anyone will be when they see what I saw!" she exclaimed. "Don't tell me you saw a tiger!" screamed Eleanor in frustration. "No, I did not. However, I did see the footprint of one! I do not know whether it was made recently or whether it is old, though," she said. The canter reversed to reveal the footprints. "I presume the footprints are fresh. Look at the moisture content in the mud," stated Margaret. "Very much. It means the tiger is somewhere here and has traversed this path recently. Therefore, please remain quiet in order to see the tiger," explained the guide. "Did you know, children, they say that even if you haven't spotted the tiger, the tiger would have definitely gotten to know of your presence," said Ms Deah. "That's just spooky, Miss!" said Amy. Thereafter, the canter proceeded cautiously and more silently than ever. However, even three hours into their drive, they did not spot anything except countless deer. Therefore, since their allotted time in the Park had almost run out, the canters stopped by a lake. That was when the first rays of sunshine had traversed millions of kilometres and penetrated the clouds to give warmth to the almost frozen children. "Ah...the heat is so lovely!" cried all the children as they could feel the warmth of the sun in each and every one of their skin cells.

On the way out of the Park and back to their resort, the children gradually took off their layers of warmth. First their earmuffs, then their caps, then their gloves and so on. By the time the canters drove into the cobbled entrance of the National Park Resort, the children were not only frozen to every joint, but also famished! Hence, they were led straight into the dining area, where they were fed with steaming, lip-smacking, flavoured beaten rice. Once everyone had gulped down their breakfast, the children were permitted to return to their rooms for some rest and to shower.

CHAPTER TWENTY

LOCAL HANDICRAFTS

For once, nobody fought for the lift as everyone wished to loosen their frozen joints. The children filed up the stairs to their respective rooms, all set to get into a warm shower.

"I was contemplating on whether I should take a bath now or not," said Margaret. "Wait. Didn't you already bathe in the morning?" asked Amber, confused. "Yes, but I want to take a shower in hot water yet again to loosen my joints," explained Margaret. "Suit yourself, then. You wanna go first? I need some time to get ready and I assume Sophie does too," replied Amber. "Sure. Thanks, Amb!" cried Margaret, grabbing her clothes and rushing into the bathroom.

Within minutes, Margaret was out of the washroom, fresh as a daisy. "Well now, that was quick!" cried Amber in shock. "As I said, Amber, I only needed to warm up my joints. I already took a full-fledged bath in the morning," justified Margaret. "I'm up next!" exclaimed Sophie. "No. Dare you go inside. I've been sitting ready for bath since much before you even began choosing your clothes, Sophie," defied Amber. "Oh, I'm sorry. I did not know that.

Well anyways, bye-bye!" cried Sophie as she scurried into the bathroom and slammed the door behind her. Amber rolled her eyes in frustration, leaving Margaret in giggles. "However, since this is your first time taking a shower on this trip, let me tell you that the water makes your toes burn!" cried Amber into the bathroom. "WHAT?!?" screamed Sophie from inside, horrified. "Don't worry, Sophie! It's not as bad as you think!" cried Margaret. "But Amber, you feel the same too? I thought that that was only for me!" exclaimed Margaret, pleased to know that she was not the one with burning toes while she bathed.

In what seemed like forever, Sophie finally came out of the bathroom, wrapped in a towel. "What took you so long? Margaret literally finished writing her diary entry, and you know how detailed her writings are!" exclaimed Amber angrily. "Sorry. As you know, I have not taken a bath for the past couple of days," justified Sophie. "That's not my problem. That was your personal choice!" snapped Amber. "Alright, alright, calm down. *Sheesh*," mumbled Sophie, approaching the bed to put on her clothes. As Margaret watched silently from the corner of the room while she sipped on warm water, chuckling softly, Amber stormed across the room with her towel and clothes hanging down her arm. In the meantime, Sophie was, in a rather lackadaisical fashion, putting her clothes on at snail's pace.

"SOPHIEEEEE!!!!!!!!" screamed Amber from inside the washroom. Margaret almost dropped her glass at the scream, and Sophie too was startled. Amber yanked the bathroom door open and stomped out of the bathroom with a frown on her face. "What happened, Amber?" asked Margaret in a supple voice. "Why don't you see for yourself, Ms Goody Shoes," said Amber, now giving Sophie a dirty look. "Oh, you come too," pointed Amber at Sophie. Sophie filed closely behind Margaret, keeping her distance from a truly infuriated Amber. Margaret stopped at the entrance to the washroom. She entered cautiously, as if to find something unprecedented, and looked about in curiosity. Finally, her eyes fixed on the ground behind the door. She stared. She giggled. "What is it?" asked Sophie. "This is it!" cried Amber, pulling Sophie behind the washroom door. As Margaret laughed to her content, Amber pointed to the ground and at the hooks of the door where Sophie had hung her used garments. "Whoops! Sorry!" cried Sophie embarrassed, grabbing her clothes and dashing out the washroom at top speed. "Oh, this girl is unbelievable, Margaret!" cried Amber, shutting the door behind Margaret as she left the washroom, still giggling.

Approximately an hour later, all the children assembled on the lawn outside the main resort building. Here, Andy briefed the children of the place they were going to be visiting: Tijur. "So children, Tijur is an NGO and has branches across the country. They support the local craftsmen – locally called *Tijur* – by creating an establishment for them to create and sell their handicrafts," explained Andy. "If you notice, there are many women too; this is an example of how they wish to empower women. First, as soon as you reach there, you will be split into 2 groups, according to your canters, and will be taken to different stations. For instance, while one group does block-printing, the other can purchase the handicrafts of their choice. I would like to remind you that all of the proceeds from your purchase will be going into supporting the poor locals' families. Since you are young, it is also my duty to remind you to take care of your belongings – especially your money. Please do not make hasty decisions or actions, for the same reason. So, all set to go?" "YES!!!"

cried the children in unison. "One more thing, children. Please remember to mind your language and behaviour. Make sure your actions do not hurt the locals at Tijur," instructed Ms Deah once all the children had boarded the coach.

Around twenty minutes into their drive, they had arrived at their destination. Tijur spread over a large area, the land covered with plantation, farms and separate buildings dedicated to a certain form of art. Although each building stood independently, they were connected by a small passage. The building at the entrance of the complex was the store where the children would be led to for purchasing the handicrafts of their choice. Once there, the children were split into two teams, like Andy had said earlier. While the students from Canter 1 proceeded towards the store, the children from Canter 2 headed towards the block-printing station.

The layout and décor of the block-printing building was in the local style. The three-storeyed building overlooked a large veranda at the centre of the roofless building, where countless clotheslines were hung with clothes drying on them. The group was further split into four semi-groups, each one led to a room where they were to try their hands at block-printing. The room was small, dark and rather stuffy with water seepage in abundance. The room was shaped as a narrow rectangle and was sparsely lit by a flickering tube light and a thin, dusty window. There was barely enough space to walk between the long rectangular table made of ancient ebony and the grey-painted walls with chipping paint. Large A3-sized sheets, block prints and paints of blue and orange-brown colours were laid on the table, just enough for all the students. Each student's sheet was uniquely decorated; while some made borders, others made abstract art. Apart from local designs, the block prints also had the large face of a tiger – the pride of the locality – and a block print saying 'National Park'. Not a single sheet did not have these prints on them.

Once they were done, the children headed out into a veranda where they hung their artwork on a clothesline to let it dry. Just as they clipped their artwork onto a clothesline, the children from Canter 1 arrived from the narrow passage that came from the store building. "So, how was it? Is it fun?" exclaimed Alice. "Oh, yes, it is!" cried Lewis. "There are also prints of a tiger's face and another one saying 'National Park'. You should definitely use those!" "Thanks!" exclaimed Alice as she walked into one of the rooms. "How is the store?" asked Margaret to Amber. "Well, it's okay, I guess. Not *that* great or anything, but what I got is truly unique. You want to see?" asked Amber excitedly. "Sure," replied Margaret, curious. Amber pulled out a large cloth bag from her backpack. "You ready? Ta-daaa!!!" exclaimed Amber as she pulled out a large stuffed bird from the bag. "What is that?" asked Margaret, taken aback. "It's a stuffed bird!" replied Amber. "Yeah, the size of *ten* average birds of the kind. Why on earth would you buy *this*?" asked Margaret, curious. "Well, my dad likes birds, so I thought I would buy him this!" exclaimed Amber. "I have no words of expression," said Margaret. "Now don't let me keep you. Go try your hands at block-printing." At this, Amber stuffed the bird back into the bag and dumped it into her backpack. Waving her hands, she filed into one of the rooms as well.

While team Canter 1 tried their hands at block-printing, team Canter 2 headed towards the store building. This building was rather simply decorated, but there were countless rooms inside it. Each room had shelves that reached up until the high ceilings, filled with handmade artifacts and handicrafts. The products ranged from little keychains to local-style clothing to laptop cases and even woven seats. There were also sharpeners and other stationery that looked like block-prints. By the time the students from Canter 2 had just explored the store, team Canter 1 was back from block-printing. They aided their friends with choosing what they should buy. Although most of the products were truly appealing to purchase, many were overpriced. For instance, a scarf that Margaret bought costed seven hundred bucks, and a single block-print that Holly bought costed five hundred. Nevertheless, the children were truly happy with their purchases. By late afternoon, the children had returned to their hotel.

"You children can sleep for a while if you wish to. You have a lot of time until your next event of the day. At half past seven, you will be meeting a former forest ranger who will tell you about his experiences and some facts about wildlife. Following that, you will be entertained by local performers who will showcase the local form of music and dance. Until then, you guys can do whatever you like," explained Ms Deah, before the children dispersed into their rooms.

The children clambered upstairs, chattering away. They had 'important' discussions as to which room each group of friends were going to meet in.

CHAPTER TWENTY-ONE

"DID YOU HEAR THAT?"

"I am going to take a bath now," said Amber. "Dare you go inside before me this time, Sophie." Margaret giggled. Sophie tucked herself under the thick, soft comforter, combing her hair. Within a few minutes, "Sophie, you can go in now!" cried Amber as she came out of bath. Sophie lazily pushed away her blanket and dragged herself across the room, towards the bathroom.

By the time the girls had completed all they had to do, it was already six o'clock. Amber sat to read on one side of the bed with the reading light on, while Margaret sat on the other side doing the same. In the meantime, Sophie rummaged through her suitcase, trying to find herself something warm to wear. "Why can I not find anything warm enough?" whined Sophie. "That's maybe because you did not pack appropriately, Sophie," said Amber cynically, rolling her eyes and giggling. "Guys, have any of you noticed that we have not done anything fun together on this trip?" said Sophie, stopping her rummaging as the reality suddenly struck her. "What do you mean? We have had a lot of fun! Remember the time you both threw the pillow on me at night? Or when Amber got upset because you had left your garments on the bathroom floor? Or the fact that we have an in-house comedian who keeps making abnormal sounds?" said Margaret, her eyes still fixed on the book that she held under the light. "True, but we should do something that is *actually* fun. For instance, why don't we prank someone?" suggested Sophie. At this, Amber shut her book and crawled towards the other edge of the bed, near Sophie. "I'm game." "How about you, Margaret?" asked Sophie. "It all depends on *what* the prank is and *who* we are pranking," replied Margaret, looking up at her roommates. "Here's the plan. Since Amber is so fabulous at making creepy noises, she will hide behind the curtains. You and I will call someone in and start a conversation on the most random topics. While we are doing so, Amber will make those classic sounds that she makes," explained Sophie. "Yes! That sounds awesome!" exclaimed Amber, excited. "Alright, the plan is nice. Who are we pranking, though?" asked Margaret. "How about Mr Bill?" suggested Sophie. "No way! I am not in a million years going to prank a teacher!" denied Margaret. "Okay, then we will prank the first student we see on our corridor. Is that okay?" asked Amber. "Sure," replied Margaret. "Will you be our welcome committee, Margaret?" asked Sophie. "Sure, why not! I have a suggestion, though. While Amber makes those sounds, we should pretend as if we cannot hear her. That way, the person we call will get even more scared," said Margaret. "Wow! For once, Margaret is doing something mischievous!" exclaimed Sophie.

The trio commenced preparing their room for the prank. Firstly, Amber and Margaret put away all of their belongings, while Sophie littered her belongings around the room. Secondly, all of the room lights were switched off.

Next, the two reading lights on either side of the bed were turned on and pointed straight at the opposite wall, which was almost four metres away. Finally, Amber hid herself behind the thick curtains, making sure she was not visible.

"Ready?" asked Sophie. "Ready," replied Margaret and Amber in unison. "I am going outside to see if there is anyone on the corridor," said Margaret, advancing towards the door. She gently turned the doorknob and peered outside. "I see one person," whispered Margaret. "Who is it?" asked Amber. "It is Kendra from Cypress," replied Margaret, closing the door behind her. "That's perfect! Will she fall for our prank, though?" asked Amber. "We won't know until we try!" cried Sophie. "Call her in."

Wrapping a shawl around her, Margaret stepped out into the cold corridors. "Kendra!" called Margaret. Kendra turned around. "Could you come here for a moment, please?" At this, Kendra sprinted across the corridor. "Yes, what happened?" asked Kendra. "Come inside," said Margaret, leading Kendra into her room.

The moment Kendra stepped into the room, Margaret slammed the door shut behind her. Kendra jerked. "Hello Kendra!!" exclaimed Sophie, pacing towards Kendra. "Umm, hi...?" replied Kendra, sensing something unusual about the vibes in the room. At seeing Kendra looking about nervously, Margaret enquired, "Is everything alright, Kendra?" "Yes, but why is your room so dark? And why is there something unusual and eerie about its vibes?" asked Kendra, noticeable fear seeping into her voice. "We're...well...we are saving electricity! You know, since our school theme for the year is sustainability," justified Sophie hastily. Right at that moment, a faint voice was heard. "Hi. I'm Suzie." "Did you hear that?" asked Kendra, startled. "Hear what?" asked Margaret. "I want to suck your blood," spoke the voice. "There it is again!" exclaimed Kendra, beginning to panic. As Kendra walked about the room to investigate, Margaret and Sophie grinned at each other. Finally, as Kendra stopped to look at the curtains, Margaret's heart paced. Sophie and Margaret exchanged tensed expressions. When Kendra popped her head into the curtain, Amber swiftly stepped out of it, winking at Margaret and Sophie who gave out a soft sigh. Just as Kendra popped her head back out, Amber slipped behind the curtains again. "What *is* happening in your room, Margaret?" asked Kendra, worried. "I think you are just imagining things," said Margaret, putting her arm around Kendra to comfort her. When she did so, she could feel Kendra's body tremble. Instantaneously, Margaret walked up to Sophie and whispered her observation into her ear. Sophie and Margaret turned around.

"Okay, well, we'll tell you what is happening," said Sophie. At this, Kendra looked at her sharply. "It was basically a prank we were playing on you." "WHAT?" cried Kendra. "Yes. And the sounds were made by Amber," said Margaret. At this, Amber stepped out from behind the curtains. All of the four girls stared at one another for a few moments. Thereafter, they dropped to the ground with laughter.

"Amber just came out of the curtains like she was a devil's spawn!" cried Kendra, laughing hysterically. "What is a devil's spawn?" asked Margaret, her hand on her stomach as she continued to laugh. "Oh yeah, what is it?" asked Amber and Sophie. "You guys seriously do not know what a devil's spawn is?!?" exclaimed Kendra in shock. The three nodded in unison. "Alright, let me demonstrate it to you." Slowly getting up with the help of a table by her side, Kendra cleared her throat. Thereafter, in an ever so dramatic way, she cried, "SO, THERE IS A DEVIL'S SPAWN AND A DEVIL'S CHILDREN. I WILL EXPLAIN THE DIFFERENCE TO YOU NOW." At this, the girls began laughing even more, for Kendra's accent was truly peculiar, with her r's rolling more than necessary and her t's being exaggerated to a level above normal.

As Kendra, laughing hysterically along with the others, began explaining the difference between 'devil's spawn' and 'devil's children', there was a knock on the door. As Sophie, Amber and Kendra continued to laugh, Margaret took a deep breath and attended to the door. It was one of Kendra's roommates. "Kendra, we need you in the room now. Hannah and Alice have fought, and now they both are crying," she explained. "Alright, I'm coming," said Kendra, trying to stop laughing. "I shall explain this to you another time," said Kendra, walking out of the door. A moment later, Margaret, Amber and Sophie burst out into a thousand laughs. "Goodness me, that sure was fun!" cried Margaret. "Yeah! You should have seen Kendra's facial expressions when she entered the room," joked Sophie. "Exactly! And the way I slipped out and back behind the curtain was hilarious too!" exclaimed Amber. Clearing her throat, Sophie said, "I shall head towards Amy, Eleanor and Laura's room now." "Sure. However, do not tell them about this yet, alright?" instructed Amber. Nodding, Sophie grabbed her comb and dashed out of the room. "My, my. Sophie and her comb!" commented Amber cynically, leaving Margaret in giggles.

"Amber, I was wondering, why don't you and I try out the same prank once again? On someone else, perhaps?" asked Margaret. "Yeah, sure! That sounds awesome! Who shall we try it on, though?" "How about Simone?" "Yeah, sure. Since she can almost be called a prank queen, we will officially be masters at pranking people if we successfully get her in the bag!" cried Amber, clapping her hands in excitement. "Yes, true. However, let us not build castles in the air just yet. Let me go fetch Simone, shall I?" "Sure, Margaret. Shall I hide behind the curtains this time as well?" asked Amber. "I really do not think Simone is as gullible as Kendra. Therefore, why don't you hide in the bathroom? I shall make sure she does not enter. If she does, just hide behind the door," explained Margaret. "Alright! Sounds cool!"

The two girls turned off all the lights except the reading lights (the same setting as before) and then proceeded towards the bathroom. Once Margaret was sure that Amber could not be easily found, she headed out of the room to find their friend Simone, who was from Cypress. Incidentally, Simone was loitering around the corridor, along with some other girls. "Simone!" called Margaret in her soft, supple voice. Simone turned to look at her. "Yes, Margaret?" she exclaimed. "Would you come here a moment, please?" asked Margaret. Simone advanced towards Margaret, nodding her head. "So, what's up, Margaret?" "Oh, I have something that I thought you may find interesting," explained Margaret, luring her target. "Really? What is it?" asked Simone, intrigued. "It is in my room. Shall we go in?" asked Margaret in an ever so friendly manner. "Sure!" cried Simone.

With a smile about to break out on Margaret's face, she turned to open the door to her room. Leading Simone inside, Margaret closed the door behind them, locking it.

Simone looked about the room suspiciously. Margaret led her friend into the room and seated her on the bed. "So, what is it that you wanted to show me?" asked Simone, still looking about sceptically. Margaret, without saying anything, unzipped her backpack and took out a small ancient-looking notebook whose cover was a woven elephant on a mauve background. Margaret unwound the red thread, that closed the book, revealing the recycled paper and the writings on them. "What is this?" asked Simone, curious. "This is called the *Brahmi* script. It is an ancient Indian script that I was researching on. This is how we write your name in this script," explained Margaret, scribbling out some symbols onto another sheet of paper. It was then that Simone's ears pricked up. "Hi there. I'm Suzie," spoke a voice. Judging the expression on Simone's face, Margaret enquired, "Is everything alright, Simone?" "Yes, partially. However, is it just me, or is this room giving out creepy vibes?" replied Simone. "Well...umm...maybe the ancient script got your imagination going wild," justified Margaret. Shrugging, Simone got her attention back to the tiny, ancient notebook. "I am really amused as to how you actually researched about this, Margaret!" cried Simone, amused.

"I smell human blood. I am hungry," spoke a soft, muffled, eerie voice. "Did you hear that?" asked Simone, terrified. "Hear what?" asked Margaret, trying to push back the smile that was struggling to come to her lips. "Can you really not hear that?" asked Simone. "No, I really cannot hear anything," replied Margaret indifferently, taking notice of the beads of sweat that were forming on Simone's forehead.

"Margaret, is there someone else in the room?" asked Simone. "No. Amber has gone downstairs to look for souvenirs, and Sophie is in Amy's room," explained Margaret, nervous of the fact that Simone was extremely close to figuring out the prank. "I don't believe you, Margaret," said Simone, getting up to investigate the room.

Margaret's heartbeat picked pace. She dumped the notebook, sheet and pen back into her backpack and scurried behind Simone. Simone peered behind the curtains, under the bed and inside the cupboard. Throughout, Amber continually made her signature sound effects. Suddenly, Simone turned to face the washroom. Margaret's heart began to pound. "I have a feeling there is somebody in there, Margaret," said Simone, inching towards the partly-open washroom door.

Inside the washroom, Amber's heart too pounded. What if Margaret failed to keep Simone out? Just at that moment, Margaret leaped ahead of Simone, blocking the entrance to the washroom. "If there was someone in my washroom, would I not be aware of it?" justified Margaret. She heard Amber's sigh from behind the door. Seeing that Simone continued to disbelieve the fact the room had one other person, Margaret said, "Alright, look at this. There is nobody here, here or here." She pointed towards the commode, the shower area and trying her best to cover Amber in the dark behind the door. "Alright, alright. Maybe I *am* hearing things," admitted Simone. At this, both Amber and Margaret sighed softly in unison. "Come on, then. Let us go downstairs. We cannot afford to be late for the speech by the retired forest ranger!" exclaimed Margaret, grabbing the room keys and Simone's hand. The two girls dashed outside the room. Simone waited as Margaret locked the door. Thereafter, they headed down the staircase. "Simone, I forgot to get my headgear. I shall just go fetch it, alright?" said Margaret, scampering back up the staircase.

Margaret unlocked their room door. She entered the room and shut the door behind her. Thereafter, she turned on the room lights. "We succeeded!" exclaimed Amber, leaping out excitedly from behind the bathroom door. The two cronies held hands and laughed their hearts out. "I almost thought you were going to leave me locked in here!" cried Amber. "Yes, I know. Now let us go downstairs. And remember – you were not in the room. You were downstairs at the souvenir store," explained Margaret. Amber nodded. Following that, the two girls grabbed their coats and slipped their headgear onto their heads.

CHAPTER TWENTY-TWO

IMPERSONATIONS

That night, after the ranger's thoroughly inspiring speech and the truly engaging music and dance performances, the children headed towards dinner.

"Children, I just need to make a quick announcement," said Ms Deah, drawing everyone's attention to her. "As you all know, we will be trekking up the National Park Fort during the early hours of tomorrow. I would like to warn you that we will come upon innumerable langur monkeys at the fort. Thus, I would strongly prohibit you from carrying *any* edible item except water in your rucksacks."

Following dinner, everyone scurried into their friends' rooms to play games and gossip until late in the night.

"Margaret, are these not Stacy's playing cards?" asked Amber, pointing at a pack of cards lying on their bed. "Yes, they are. We best return them to her," replied Margaret. "How did they land here, though? Stacy never came to the room," wondered Amber. "Perhaps Sophie brought them with her from Stacy's room?" suggested Margaret. "Yes, probably." Thereafter, the girls pulled a sweater over their night suits and headed into the corridor, locking their room door behind them.

Incidentally, Stacy was out on the corridor with a bunch of people. Hence, Margaret handed the cards over to her. Thanking them, Stacy took the cards and scurried into one of the rooms. Almost instantly, almost everyone disappeared from the corridor – except Alice. Amber and Margaret exchanged sceptical glances at the occurrence. Thereafter, they turned back towards their room. Suddenly, they heard a cry. They turned around, only to see Alice on all fours with her hair falling over her face. The cronies inched backwards, their eyes fixed on their classmate, Alice. All of a sudden, Alice jerked her head up, causing her hair to fly back. She then began racing towards Amber and Margaret, crawling on her knees and elbows. Amber and Margaret, shrieking, dashed towards their room. Margaret's hands trembled as she tried to unlock their room door hastily. Amber was squealing behind her, begging her to open the door quicker. Finally, when the door opened, the two girls clambered in. They fell to the ground in fear. Just as Alice approached their door, Margaret slammed it shut and locked it.

"Oh, my goodness! What was that?" cried Margaret, lending her hand to Amber who was still on the floor. "CATASTROPHE!" cried Amber, clutching her friend's palm as she got off the ground. The two girls burst out into a thousand laughs. "Thank goodness you closed the door on time. Otherwise, can you imagine all the drama she would have caused *inside* the room?" said Amber, still laughing.

Later in the night, the room was peaceful and quiet. While Amber sat on the bed reading a story of Sherlock Holmes that she had downloaded on her iPod, Margaret was writing an account of all that happened that day. The only sound in the room, therefore, was of Margaret scribbling in her diary. All of a sudden, the room intercom rang. "I wonder who that could be," said Margaret, walking up to the bedside to answer the call. "Hello?" asked Margaret, as Amber looked at her intently. "Hello ma'am, this is hotel reception. I believe you ordered a hot chocolate?" Margaret's forehead creased. "Who is it, Margaret?" asked Amber, curious. "It was someone claiming to be hotel reception. She asked whether I had ordered hot chocolate," replied Margaret, putting down the phone. "I reckon that was our Amy from the other room," stated Margaret, returning to the study at the other end of the room. "The next time they call, let me answer, alright?" Margaret nodded.

Just then, the phone rang again. Amber crawled towards the other end of the bed at top speed. She picked up the phone. Margaret watched intently as Amber listened. Suddenly, Amber spoke, "In the year 1878, I took my degree of Doctor of Medicine of the University of London, proceeded to Netley to go through the course prescribed for surgeons in the army. Having completed my studies there, I was duly attached to the Fifth Northumberland Fusiliers as Assistant Surgeon. The regiment was stationed in India at the time, and before I could join it, second Afghan war had broken out." Amber then put down the phone, only to find Margaret bursting out into a hysteric laughter. "WHAT WAS THAT?" asked Margaret. "It was the first chapter from the Sherlock Holmes story I am reading," explained Amber, crawling back to the other side of the bed. "Oh Amber, you are just so funny!" exclaimed Margaret. Margaret's eyes suddenly fell to the black-strapped watch she had around her right wrist. "It is already ten o'clock. We'd best be in bed. We have to go trekking tomorrow!" said Margaret, putting away her diary and stationery. Amber too shut down her iPod and packed it into her suitcase. "One of us will have to stay awake until Sophie comes," said Amber. "True. However, if she does not come within the next ten minutes, you can have fun awaiting her," replied Margaret.

Just then, the doorbell rang. "Phew! I think that is Sophie!" exclaimed Amber as Margaret rushed to the door. When she pulled the lever to open the door, she was greeted by Ms Deah and Mr Bill. "Hello, my dear," said Mr Bill. "I trust all three of you are in here?" asked Ms Deah. "Sophie isn't yet here, Ms Deah," replied Margaret politely. "Oh. Well, in that case, do you or Amber happen to know where she is?" asked Ms Deah. "I think she is in the neighbouring room," called Amber. "Very well. We shall send her here." Just as Ms Deah said that, the intercom rang. Gesturing Margaret not to answer the phone, Ms Deah rushed into the room to answer the call. Margaret and Mr Bill came around the corner as well, joining Amber at watching Ms Deah with much curiosity. "Yes, yes. They are here right now. I will tell them," whispered Ms Deah into the phone, putting it down. "What happened, Ms Deah?" asked Amber. "Nothing. I shall send Sophie in here momentarily," replied Ms Deah indifferently, striding out of the room with Mr Bill following closely. Amber and Margaret looked at one another, shrugged and turned away. Within moments, the doorbell rang yet again. It was Sophie, escorted by Ms Deah and Mr Bill on either side. Taking Sophie into the room, Margaret wished the teachers a good night and then shut the door.

"Why did you tell them, Margaret?" asked Sophie, frustrated. "Tell who what?" asked Margaret, confused. "Why did you tell Ms Deah and Mr Bill that I was in the bathroom of Amy's room?" asked Sophie, jumping onto the bed. "Oh, I did not answer the phone," said Margaret, causing Sophie's expression to change into that of confusion. "Then who was it who answered Amy's call?" asked Sophie, puzzled. "It was Ms Deah," replied Margaret. "WHAT?!" exclaimed Sophie. "Wait a minute. What did Amy tell on the phone?" asked Amber. "Amy called you up to say that you must tell the teachers that I am in fact in the bathroom and not in their room so that I would not get caught," clarified Sophie. "Oh, no!" cried Amber and Margaret in unison. "Trust me, though, you and Ms Deah sound exactly alike – especially when you are whispering on the phone," said Sophie. "What did Ms Deah say when she came to that room?" asked Amber, curious. "Nothing much. She simply asked whether I was in the washroom," replied Sophie, chuckling.

"Anyhow, let us get to bed. We have a long day ahead of us!" cried Margaret, turning off the lights.

CHAPTER TWENTY-THREE

"IS THAT A TIGER?"

The next morning, everyone joked about the incident of Ms Deah impersonating Margaret the previous night. Soon, the children and teachers were aboard their respective canters and had set off for the National Park Fort which was situated within the National Park.

The children had a dandy time trekking up the fort and listening to the fascinating yet tragic stories of the ancient royals that once resided in the fort. Now, however, the fort was left in ruins. Enroute, the children even encountered a group of politicians, clad in white, who insisted on taking a photograph along with the children. As they climbed up the ancient rock steps, the children realised that their teachers had vanished! After an hour of hunting, the children finally reunited with their teachers.

At around 3 PM, after lunch, everyone set off for the National Park yet again. This time, they intended to explore zones 4 and 5. After a long, chilly drive in the dry, dusty forest, somebody shrieked, "Is that a tiger?!" Following the direction she pointed to, everyone's eyes fell upon a valley. The valley had small masses of land covered in lush-green grass sprinkled on a vast lake whose water shimmered in the setting sun. On the land right at the foot of the mountain, there were three deep-blue peacocks standing with their feathers flared out. These three peacocks, however, stood dead still and stared intently at one of the islands. Following the path of the peacocks' eyes, the children's eyes spotted a striped figure lying amidst the tall grass. The children spent approximately half an hour observing the tiger, watching it get up to sip water from the lake and then laze in the sun again.

The children drove contently back to the hotel, chewing on sweet and juicy guavas that their resort had especially packed for them.

By the time they were at the hotel, the children and their chaperones were covered in dust from head to toe. "You children best change your clothes and wash your hair," said Ms Deah as everyone descended from the canters, exhausted from all the excitement. "But first..." said Ms Deah, pointing towards a large container that was placed at the centre of the hotel yard. The container was filled with noodles! The children raced towards the container, picked their cutlery and fell in line to get some of the lip-smacking Maggi noodles. Alongside, they were served piping hot chocolate.

"All of you can spend some time in your rooms – maybe rest or just chill. Following that, please head back to the yard by half past seven for the dance party!" exclaimed Ms Deah.

That evening, the children had a blast at the dance party! The music was blaring at full volume, and the yard was lit with multicoloured disco lights. Towards the end of the party, each student was awarded with a *Junior Rangers Programme – Certificate of Participation* and was expected to speak a few words expressing their overall feelings of the trip. What a wonderful way to end the trip!

After dinner, everyone mournfully climbed up the hotel staircase and onto their corridor, wishing for the night to last longer. "Guys!" called Mr Bill, out of the blue. "We teachers have decided that you can stay up until eleven, considering that this is the last day of our trip." After a moment of silence, "YAY!!" All the children cried in unison, jubilantly promenading into their friends' rooms.

By eleven o'clock, all the children were in their respective rooms. However, nobody was asleep as yet. As the teachers patrolled the hallway, they could hear chatters from some rooms and clammers from others. Mr Bill, therefore, went door to door warning the children to get to sleep. "Please get to sleep," he called at Margaret, Amber and Sophie's room. In a few minutes, when the girls continued to stay awake, "Margaret, Sophie, Amber: this is your final warning. If you still do not sleep, you are going to be in *deep* trouble." Although his deep, muffled voice sounded hilarious, the children fell silent and asleep at once. Similarly, he warned all those who hadn't yet slept.

Early next morning, Margaret awoke an hour earlier than the others, as usual. Once she was ready, she began putting away her alarm clock, toiletries, garments, towels, winter wear and all her other possessions. By the time she had finished, the doorbell rang. "Good morning! Rise and shine, children!" called Ms Deah. It was their wake-up call. Therefore, Margaret woke her roommates up.

In half an hour, all the students had lined up their suitcases in front of their awaiting coach and proceeded for breakfast. Once they had gulped down their scrumptious meal, all the students and teachers promenaded on the yard. They made the most of their last few minutes at the hotel, breathing out more air than usual so as to enjoy the feel of the 'smoke' coming out of their mouths due to the cold. Soon, everyone was aboard the coach and bidding goodbye to their resort. During the bus ride, almost everyone crowded around Mr Bill, who was watching an anime movie on his phone.

Within a little over four hours, they had arrived at the main city from where they were to catch their flight back home. Before the airport, however, they broke at McDonalds. "Since this is going to be the last meal of your trip," explained Andy, "we have decided to treat you by taking you to McDonalds." The children jubilantly got off the coach and strode towards McDonalds. However, many of the children were much disappointed as the meals served were vegetarian. Nevertheless, they crunched down the salty French fries, gobbled up the cheesy burger and gulped down the fizzy coke. Following their meal, all the students and teachers posed for a photograph, holding up the McDonalds paper goggles. Funny enough, this was at the request of the McDonalds staff themselves!

At the airport, unlike during their journey from home, the children had to check in their baggage themselves. Therefore, everyone filed in front of the counter with their bags, impatiently awaiting their turn. Once everyone had finished checking in their respective luggage, each was given a food box to relish at the airport, on the flight, or at home. While these boxes were being handed out, some of the air hostesses of their airline requested a picture with the children. The children readily consented. "Wow, kids! You guys have become celebrities over this trip. First politicians, then McDonalds and now flight crew!" commented Ms Lancy as they headed towards their boarding gate.

On the flight and on their drive home, the children relived every moment of this absolutely mesmerising field trip, cherishing the memories they had made together with their friends and teachers.

CHAPTER TWENTY-FOUR

STUDENT TROUBLE!

No matter how 'innocent' or 'sweet' children may be, the students of Magnolia had crossed all boundaries with regards to following rules. They swore, chewed on gum, left their hair untied, wore incorrect uniforms and back answered teachers. It was almost evident that no teacher enjoyed teaching the Magnolians for it was definite that they would be teased and/or insulted.

One day, during the mathematics class, Ms Hendricks was teaching volume and surface area of composite figures. Towards the end of class, Adam required some assistance from Ms Hendricks. Therefore, she was helping him solve a question. Meanwhile, Jake was speaking loudly – in fact almost screaming – about their field trip. Since his speech was an obvious disturbance for Ms Hendricks, she raged at him. "Jake! Why are you speaking at such a high volume? I am not able to hear what Adam is telling me, and I myself am being compelled to scream," she said. Jake replied, "Alright Ms Hendricks, don't scream." At this, the entire class burst out laughing. Furious, Ms Hendricks replied, "You are the class representative. You must be a role model for the rest of your class – not be a part of their mischief!"

The next lesson was world language. All the pupils of the grade dispersed to their respective world language classrooms, the options being Spanish, French and Hindi. One boy from Cypress, named George, was chatting along with his other friends during their French class. As Mr Monaghan – the French teacher – was teaching the students *Passé Composé*, he was repeatedly interrupted by George's loud, baritone voice that echoed across the class. At first, Mr Monaghan gave George gentle warnings, trying to fan off his brewing anger. However, despite innumerable warnings, George continued to chatter away with his friends. Suddenly, out of the blue, the entire class jerked. "GEORGE! I have repeatedly warned you to be silent, yet you decide to test my patience! I hope you realise that I can kick you out of the window as if you were a football. In fact, it is not just you. Your entire class is like wild horses in the middle of a jungle! Be it you, Alice, Kendra or Hannah, all of you keep talking while I am teaching. What *AUDACITY* do you have to do so, disrespecting a teacher so? Please keep in mind that there are people in this class, like Thomas, Margaret, Eleanor and more, who actually *want* to learn. However, due to the misbehaviour of some people in a class, the entire class is deprived of knowledge. Please behave yourselves, children! You are in Middle School – please remember that."

At the same time, the children of Magnolia had multifaceted talents. Be it dance, music, theatre, art, sports or academics, the teachers could always rely on a Magnolian to step forward for participation.

CHAPTER TWENTY-FIVE

THE VENKATESH FAMILY

One gloomy Thursday morning in the month of February, the students of Magnolia filed into class, barely able to walk with heavy bags mounted on their shoulders. As each student set their bag on the floor beneath their respective tables, one could hear a loud 'THUD', indicating the weight of the bag. The process of children sauntering into the classroom and then dropping the dead weight of their bags onto the ground continued.

As Margaret sat at her place right in front of the teacher's table, she awaited the arrival of Ms Lancy for CTP (class teacher's period). While doing so, she gazed up at the lizard – Mani Venkatesh – who was perched up on the clock. "Why does he look smaller today, though?" thought Margaret. Suddenly, the lizard fell off the wall. Seeing that nobody had noticed this yet, Margaret silently observed the lizard. She inferred that the lizard had lost the suction property that its feet possessed. She then looked back up at the clock, from where the lizard had fallen. Surprisingly, Mani was still up there! So, who was *this*?

Right at that moment, Luke exclaimed, "Look, guys! Mani Venkatesh has fallen!" At this, almost the entire class raced towards the spot where the lizard was scampering about in circles, making no attempts of climbing back up the wall. "This is not Mani," stated Margaret. The class silenced. "Mani is in fact still up there in his abode – at the clock." Saying this, Margaret pointed up to where Mani Venkatesh was. "Oh! Well in that case, this might be his girlfriend, Mary Venkatesh!" exclaimed Lewis. "Yeah!" cried the class in unison. Luke, thinking on his feet, dragged a spare chair towards Mary. Thereafter, he cornered 'her' using it. Just then, Ms Lancy walked into the class for CTP. "Ms Lancy! Look who we found here! It is Mary Venkatesh, Mani Venkatesh's girlfriend!" cried Jake excitedly, pointing at Mary. At the sight of a lizard on the ground, Ms Lancy winced, shivering in fear. Reflexively, Ms Lancy stepped back. After taking the attendance, she fled from the class at top speed.

Throughout the rest of the day, Mary Venkatesh continually scampered about in circles, remaining within the shadow of the massive piece of furniture above her. While most of the teachers ignored the lizard, some feared it. Others, namely Mr Bill, wished for its freedom. "What you guys have done is not correct, kids. We should let her free. Alice, could you bring me a piece of paper please?" At this, Alice brought Mr Bill a piece of paper. Thereafter, Mr Bill fearlessly scooped up the lizard on the paper, strode towards the window and defenestrated it. "NO!!" cried Luke, Lewis and some other Mary Venkatesh lovers. "Her freedom is much more important than your pleasure, children." Saying this, Mr Bill indifferently began his class. However, the memories of Mary Venkatesh remained forever in the hearts of every Magnolian and, undoubtedly, in the heart of her beloved Mani Venkatesh.

Within a few days, the Magnolians – and hopefully Mani Venkatesh as well – had recovered from the loss incurred upon them. One day, Margaret and Amber were walking up the stairs to the third floor. The third floor was Margaret's favourite place in the school as the school's physics and chemistry laboratories were situated on this floor. Sandwiched between the two labs, however, stood a *GIANT* Periodic Table of Elements. This table covered the space of the entire wall, and the entire table could be lit up according to the groups and periods. It was Margaret's pastime to go up to the third floor and gaze at the Periodic Table and/or the laboratories. Thus, the two cronies were walking up from their classroom, which was two floors below the Periodic Table. Suddenly, somewhere near the landing of the second floor, Amber pointed towards the railing and wore an expression of horror. Looking at what Amber was pointing to, Margaret shrieked as well. It was a tiny lizard! "That's Lizzy – Mani and Mary Venkatesh's long-lost daughter," declared Amber.

Soon after, the news of Lizzy spread like wildfire in Magnolia. "Well, we can look up to Lizzy to take over her father's position once he is too old," joked Luke.

For the time being, Mani Venkatesh was thoroughly pampered. Every day, somebody or the other would praise Mani as if he were a prodigy or a luminary. Or, as if he were God, looking down on all of the world and blessing it. The teachers too had begun acknowledging the presence of the much-celebrated lizard. Very soon, he was established as the official class pet of Magnolia.

One sunny lunch break, when the blazing sun was scorching as if it were a pool of golden snakes glistening in the sky and slithering in circles, all of the girls and boys from Magnolia and Cypress were seated in their respective groups, gossiping as they munched their lunch. Once they had finished eating, Margaret and Amber were strolling about the school. They were walking down the Elementary School corridor when their eyes fell upon a much-desired sight. It was Lizzy Venkatesh! She was perched on a metal grill which was fixed to prevent children falling off. Just as Amber and Margaret raced towards Lizzy in excitement, Lizzy's suction gave way as well, causing Lizzy to fall through the holes in the large metal grill and onto the ground of the floor below. "I can imagine why Lizzy did so. Imagine, Margaret, the poor girl's mother was defenestrated and her father has been held hostage in our classroom," explained Amber, looking sombrely at the wall where Lizzy was a few seconds ago. "I can empathise with her. Poor dear," said Margaret.

The girls then informed the rest of Magnolia about this tragedy they had just encountered. All the sounds of laughter and cynicism were replaced by a deep, haunting wave of melancholy and sorrow. The teachers were truly taken aback by this sudden calmness in the Magnolia classroom. However, nobody explained the reason behind this mysterious silence.

CHAPTER TWENTY-SIX

THE MOCKERY SHOW

"As the volume decreases, the pressure increases. Let me give you an example. Consider this a cylinder," explained Mr Richard, drawing a cylinder and a piston on the whiteboard. "Imagine that the space between the piston and the base of the cylinder is filled with air. Now, when I push this piston down...oops! This marker has run out of ink!" The marker indeed was spitting out its last words of cry. Therefore, Margaret handed over another marker to Mr Richard. "Thanks, Margaret. So, as I was saying, if this piston is pushed downwards, the volume of the air is decreasing. Hence, there are more collisions between the particles in the continually decreasing area. And in turn, as we had learned in the last class, the pressure increases as the number of collisions increases. So, let us write down the statement: when the volume decreases, pressure increases."

As Mr Richard reached halfway through the statement, the marker ran out of ink. "Do you have another one, Margaret?" Margaret dug through her pencil case and took out a marker. Mr Richard tried out the marker, but its ink had dried up as well. Margaret took out yet another marker, and another, and another, all of which had no ink in them. "Does your class have any working markers at all?" asked Mr Richard cynically, trying out another marker that Margaret had given him. Finally, the seventh marker that Margaret gave Mr Richard wrote as if it were brand new. Before continuing to write the statement, Mr Richard said, "Margaret, have you ever thought of opening a stationery shop? You have adequate stationery for the entire school!" At this, the class burst out laughing.

Later into the class, Mr Richard was waiting for the children to finish taking down the notes so that he could resume teaching. Finally, once the children had finished, Mr Richard advanced towards the whiteboard, shushing the class. "Guys, be quiet! Don't talk like Alice and Margaret." At this, the entire class gasped. "OH-MY-GOD," cried the entire class. "Margaret spoke in class?!?" "Guys, calm down. Margaret is also human," said Ben. "Yeah, guys, exactly," said Mr Richard in a sarcastic tone. "I mean, she *looks* human. However, *is* she human?" Margaret smiled.

Later the same day, Ms Fernandes came to Magnolia for their biology class. "Alright, kids, may I have your attention?" called Ms Fernandes. "I am going to ask you guys a few questions as a revision of what we learned last class. The first question is: what is an example of manmade ecosystems?" At this, a majority of the class raised their hands, eager to answer this question that was a piece of cake. "Yes, Alice?" "Miss, it is the rice paddy." "Very good, Alice. The next question is: what is osteoporosis? Can you answer, Harry?" Nodding, Harry answered, "Osteoporosis is a deficiency disease due to the lack of vitamin D where the bones develop holes in them and become brittle." "Good, Harry. One point you can add is that the bone density decreases. Now, Adam, could you explain to me the difference between biomagnification and bioaccumulation?" After taking a moment to think, Adam replied, "While bioaccumulation is the gradual build-up of toxic substances in the body, biomagnification is the increase in concentration of a substance as one goes up the food chain." "Nicely worded, Adam!" At that moment, Ms Fernandes' eyes fell upon Lewis who was gazing at the ceiling. "Lewis, are you in love?" asked Ms Fernandes suddenly. At this, the entire class burst out into a roar of unstoppable laughter. "Of course not, Miss!" defended an embarrassed Lewis. "Then why are you daydreaming?" asked Ms Fernandes. "It's nothing, Ms Fernandes," replied Lewis. After staring at him suspiciously for a few seconds, Ms Fernandes returned to her quiz.

"Now that we have revised our topics, everyone please give me your notebooks. While I check them, can you all take out the revision worksheet that I had given you? Those who have already done it, please check your answers. Those who haven't, please do it now and then check your answers," instructed Ms Fernandes. "What do we check with, miss?" asked Eleanor. "Margaret, can you write down the answers to the worksheet on the whiteboard please?" After receiving a marker from Ms Fernandes, Margaret began writing the answers to the worksheet on the whiteboard. Just then, there was a knock on the door. "Ms Fernandes, could I speak to you for a moment please?" asked Ms Elizabeth, who was at the door. Therefore, Ms Fernandes left the classroom telling her students to remain quiet and behave. However, could she really expect that out of Magnolians?

The moment Ms Fernandes left the classroom, the children began chattering. Then, Luke said mockingly, "Ms Margaret, could you check my work please? Are my answers correct?" At this, the entire class burst into laughter. Margaret turned around, gave Luke a sly look, and turned back towards the board. Next, Jake joked, "Ms Margaret, do you want a chair?" "Yes! You are so short; you definitely need a chair!" commented Luke. Margaret replied politely, remaining calm, "Oh, I truly appreciate how much my beloved class cares for me, but thank you very much – I can manage pretty well without a chair." After a few chuckles, Adam stated, "You do, Margaret, actually look like a teacher." "Why, thank you, Adam," replied Margaret. Just then, Ms Fernandes returned to the class. She continued correcting the notebooks. Luke spoke again, "Ms Margaret, would you like a chair?" This time, Margaret did not turn around – she simply continued writing on the board, nodding side-to-side as if to say, "You will never improve." While Margaret took it casually, Ms Fernandes smelled something fishy. "What are they making fun of, Margaret?" Margaret turned and said, "They are making fun of my height, Ms Fernandes." Ms Fernandes glared at Luke. Thereafter, she spoke, "You children ought to be polite to your peers and teachers. Someone's height is not in their hands, is it?" "However, a lot of space is getting wasted at the top of the whiteboard, miss! We are not able to proceed forward quickly," complained Jake. "Well, in that case, erase everything from the whiteboard, Margaret. They have finished it already, isn't it? Hence, you can move ahead." Therefore, Margaret followed her teacher's instructions. Thereafter, the class struggled to keep up with Margaret's pace. However, little did Ms Fernandes budge.

The next day, Magnolia had geography as their first lesson. Starting from that day, High School had their final exams. Since Ms Anne also taught geography to High school, she was called to one of the exam rooms as one of the children had a query regarding the paper. Therefore, leaving Margaret and Jake in charge, she left the classroom.

The moment she left, however, all the children took their respective positions. Two boys were stationed at the door, standing guard in order to alert the rest of their class if any teacher was passing their class. They closed all the windows and drew the blinds. Simultaneously, a group of students, led by Alice, turned on the class computer. Connecting it to the speaker, they played music on full volume. As and when a teacher happened to pass by the classroom, the music would be paused. The moment the coast was clear, it would begin again. Not only was there music playing, but the students were also dancing. Some students, like Alice, Ben and Jamie, danced to the music in full swing. Others, like Thomas, Eleanor, Laura, Sophie and Amy, grooved and vibed to the music. The remaining, like Margaret and Amber, simply sat at their seats, helpless. Margaret had, at first, made an attempt to convince her peers not to do so. However, since she was clearly a minority in her opinion, she was forced to return to her seat.

Momentarily, Ms Anne returned to the class. She enquired with them about the source of the music. While all of the class remained silent, Margaret spilled the beans. After hearing an earful, the class fell silent, boiling in anger at Margaret.

CHAPTER TWENTY-SEVEN

A DISASTROUS BRIDGE

Every Tuesday, Middle School had afterschool clubs until half past 3. There were club options for music, art, dance, debate, environment, outreach and science. Every week or two, the clubs would take on a new project to work on.

One such Tuesday, Mr Richard, Ms Delilah (the chemistry teacher) and one other physics teacher – the teachers who conducted the science club – had given the students a project of creating a bridge using popsicle sticks. "Here are some ideas of girders that you could use in the fabrication of your bridge," said Mr Richard as he handed out sheets of paper having the designs of girders. "You can sketch your truss pattern on this grid. Then, you can place your popsicle sticks on it and glue them together at the nodes," he explained. Margaret, Amber and Laura were grouped together, along with three younger Middle Schoolers. Margaret carefully studied the sheet. Finally, after much contemplation, she spoke, "How about we do the Pennsylvania pattern? Or what about Fink?" As Margaret pointed to the designs she was proposing to use in their bridge, the others' eyes popped out of their eye sockets at the sight of the much-complicated patterns. "Or, Margaret, how about we do something like this – the Warren pattern," intervened Laura. The Warren pattern was a set of triangles that were connected at the top and bottom. "Is this not a little too simple, though?" asked Margaret, not too satisfied. "Nah…as long as we get it done neatly and in time, I don't suppose it should matter," said Laura. "Yeah, fair point," she agreed.

The teams spent the rest of the time they had in sketching out their design roughly on a sheet of paper. Some more optimistic teams had already begun gluing their popsicle sticks together. By half past three, all the teams had a vague, if not vivid, idea of what they wished their bridges to look like. Keeping the partly done projects in their lockers or in the Middle School science lab, the children proceeded towards their respective buses after grabbing some snacks for themselves.

The next week, the children gathered yet again to continue working on their projects. This week, however, none of the teams got much work done. Likewise, the children continued to procrastinate for the next few weeks.

Finally, five weeks after the project was given, the children had yet to finish their respective bridges. "Children, this is not acceptable. We had given you this project weeks ago, yet not a single one of you are even close to completing your respective bridges," said Ms Delilah, furious. "If you aren't done with your projects by next Tuesday, we will move to the next project. Don't forget that your projects are being graded."

The next week, however, none of the teams had completed their projects. While some had completed their girders, others had completed their structures. However, as a whole, nobody was finished. At this, all the three teachers were furious.

"Guys, if you continue to behave like this, what is the point of us having these clubs? These clubs are meant to learn something new – maybe a skill, maybe some concept, maybe anything. However, unless you embrace this opportunity that we are giving you to learn, how are you going to learn?" explained Mr Richard. "As redemption," explained Ms Delilah, "each one of you has to come up with something innovative before the next week. Those who cannot make a model can even suffice with a poster. However, everyone *has* to make something or the other. The topic can be of your own choice."

All said and done, barely two children brought projects the next week. While Margaret brought a poster & model of Maglev trains, a girl from one of the lower grades brought a DC generator.

A Truly Humiliating Assembly

Somewhere towards the beginning of February, it was Magnolia's turn to perform for the morning assembly. However, unlike under normal circumstances, the Activities Team did not provide them with a theme; it was left at their disposal. Therefore, many CTPs were spent contemplating on the theme for the assembly.

Finally, one CTP, Ms Lancy announced, "Children, since you are unable to come up with a theme for the assembly, how about I suggest one?" At this, the children looked up at her intently. Therefore, she turned around and wrote on the board in big, bold letters: **PEER PRESSURE**. "PEER PRESSURE?!?!" the class exclaimed in unison. Ms Lancy was taken aback at this sudden uprise. "Miss, how can we do an assembly on peer pressure? It is such a vague and boring topic to perform on," complained one of the Magnolians. "Yes, I know. However, do you have any other suggestions?" At this statement by Ms Lancy, the class fell silent. "So, what other choice do we have?"

The very next day, the class got to work. They had planned to put up a script (written by Margaret) and a group song ('Believer' by Imagine Dragons) by the entire class. Alongside, some of the more artistic children were to make posters related to peer pressure and display them about the school – in the corridors, outside the classrooms, on the noticeboards.

Although the play was well scripted and the song was well rehearsed, the final programme was nothing short of an eight-letter word: DISASTER.

The actors' voices were not audible as they had not asked for microphones; the guitar & drums were overpowering the singers; the voices of barely a singer or two were audible. However, the children and Ms Lancy were satisfied with the fact that they had at least attempted.

CHAPTER TWENTY-NINE

THE BOARD OF OPERATIONS, MAGNOLIA

Towards the middle of March, the Magnolians had got into more trouble than average. Almost all the teachers had complained about Magnolia to Ms Lancy and/or Ms Elizabeth.

Finally, one day, the teachers got fed up with the children of Magnolia. Therefore, Ms Elizabeth and Ms Lancy decided to have a word with the children.

"Children, this is the limit. There is not a single teacher who has not complained about you. If it's not misbehaviour, it is rude or inappropriate language. Multiple students, even from other grades, have voiced their concerns against you to me," explained Ms Elizabeth. "You have to remember that you are now in Middle School and that you must strive to be a role model for your juniors, not someone they look down upon. This lackadaisical behaviour is simply unacceptable and will not be tolerated any longer. In another few years, you will be in High School and then college. Thus, it is imperative that you know how to conduct yourselves well." As Ms Elizabeth spoke, the room was so silent that even the movement of a muscle was audible. Ms Lancy stood at the hind corner of the classroom with a frown on her face, disappointed with her children. The children too listened attentively and did not interrupt, unlike usually.

Soon after, Ms Elizabeth concluded her address to the children. Although the students awaited disappointed remarks from Ms Lancy as well, Ms Lancy simply walked out of the classroom behind Ms Elizabeth. This deeply impacted the children.

Just before lunch, the children gathered in the classroom for a class meeting. All other students were prohibited from entering the classroom. The children shut the door, closed the windows and drew the blinds.

"We need to talk," stated Luke. Eleanor rolled her eyes. "Yes, everyone. As you heard, our class does not have the best reputation currently. Hence..." before Margaret could finish, Luke snapped, "Cut the grammar, Margaret. We need to get better, basically. We have to improve our behaviour – at least until we win a Best Class Award. So, what we need to do is stop back answering teachers, stop screaming across the corridors and keep our classroom clean. No exceptions whatsoever." At this, Alice replied, "Very true, Luke. However, how about you execute what you just said instead of preaching others?" "Alright guys, quit the blame game. Let us get to action," interfered Margaret, cutting the argument at the correct time and preventing a violent quarrel from taking place.

"Alright. Let us form a Board," said Luke, after silent moments of much contemplation. "A Board? What do you mean?" asked Margaret. "Like how our school has a Board, let us form a Board too. This Board will be in charge of the administration of our class, like in the school," explained Luke. "Alright!" agreed Jake. "So, the Board will comprise of myself, Jake, Alice, Hannah, Ben and Lewis. If anyone has to be added or removed, it shall happen in due course. The president of our Board will be Margaret since she is one of the class representatives," elaborated Luke. "How about Jake? He is also a class representative," asked Margaret. "Nah, I'm not worth it," stated Jake blatantly. All excited, Luke uttered, "We also need to make a rules chart and a suggestions chart, not to mention a lost-and-found and a bottle station." As Luke spoke, Eleanor and Laura escaped the room, bored and hungry. Not long after their escape, the class meeting was dispersed.

After lunch, Amber and Margaret sauntered up to their class for water. Much to their surprise, they were greeted by the newly elected 'Board', who were deeply involved in drafting the rules chart and clearing up the cluttered classroom.

"Margaret! I'm glad you're here. Could you please tell us the rules we need to put on the chart? Sophie has volunteered to do the writing, so all you have to do is tell us the rules," called Luke. "Margaret!" cried Ben from the other end of the class. "Is this suggestions chart looking good?" Then suddenly, Lewis dragged Margaret by the hand, taking her to the hind corner of the classroom (behind the structural pillar) where the shelf and their nonfunctional air cooler stood. "Look, Margaret!" he cried. "We have made a lost-and-found and a bottle station," explained Lewis, pointing at the shelf which had a hanging poster on it that read 'LOST & FOUND' and the table beside it on which stood a dozen water bottles. "Wow. A lot has changed in twenty minutes," said Margaret, sharing glances of astonishment with Amber.

"Margaret! The rules chart is ready!" cried Luke from the other end of the class, gesturing Margaret to have a look at it. Margaret, followed by Amber, approached Luke and Sophie. She then looked at the poster intently. After a few seconds, she spoke, "Where is the rule that says 'No chewing gum'?" At this, Luke said with utmost confidence, "Oh, we scrapped that rule. I cannot deny teenagers the pleasures they deserve." "However, if we wish to improve, must we not improve completely? No exceptions, remember?" argued Margaret. "Yeah, but this is not an exception – it's a right," said Luke, giggling as he walked away.

"So, shall I put this up, Maggie?" asked Sophie. "*Maggie*?!" exclaimed Amber and Margaret in unison. "Oh, right," called Luke from the back of the class. "I have made nicknames for everyone. You, Margaret, are Maggie; Amber is Amb; Adam is Ad; Ben is Benny Boy; Eleanor is Ellie; Amy is...I guess Amy itself; Jake is Junky and so on," explained Luke.

"Oh, and one more thing, Margaret: we have decided that this is going to be a litter-free zone. Therefore, even if there is any litter on the floor, whoever sees it will pick it up. Same thing for the lights and fans," stated Lewis. "We don't have to say those things to Margaret. She goes about switching off the lights and fans of other classrooms as well," said Amber. "Why on earth would you do that, Maggie?" asked Sophie. "Actually, I don't really care. Shall I put up this poster now?" Margaret nodded in agreement.

Just then, the bell rang. Instantly, all the children took their respective seats. Just then, Ms Delilah walked in for her lab class. "Hello class," she said as she walked in. "Today, we shall not go to the lab, but we will work with molecule models. Essentially, we will be creating models of molecules like those of water, carbon dioxide and methane," she explained.

Further into the class, when she saw that the pupils were listening attentively and not interrupting or creating havoc as they usually did, she felt suspicious. "Is everything alright? Did none of you eat lunch?" Taking this as an opportunity to brag, Luke spoke, "Miss, we as a class aspire to win the Best Class Award." At this, Eleanor rolled her eyes, leaving Margaret in chuckles. "We are striving to improve our behaviour and our infrastructure. See, miss," Luke got up, ready to give his chemistry teacher a tour of their class doings. "This is the lost-and-found, this is the place where everyone will keep their bottles, this is the rules chart and this is the suggestions chart. Finally, we have also created a Board of Operations which will manage the class. The President of the Board of Operations of Magnolia is none other than our very own Margaret whom we will henceforth refer to as 'Maggie'." Listening to all of this, Ms Delilah's eyes almost fell off their sockets.

"What has happened to your class, Margaret?" she asked after a few moments of processing. "All of this is *because* of Margaret, Ms Delilah. She has always been telling us that we must be a role model for our youngsters and that we should be worthy of being looked up to. However, we never heeded her words until Ms Elizabeth reiterated these exact words earlier today. Hence, Ms Delilah, we would be ever so grateful if you could consider voting Magnolia for the Best Class Award." Listening to Luke's speech, Ms Delilah was in tears of laughter. "I will certainly consider, my dear Luke. All the best for your endeavour," said Ms Delilah.

In contrast to the common anticipation, this meticulous care towards the class and its welfare continued for days to follow. However, all those who were not part of the Board – including Amber, Thomas, Adam, Eleanor, Laura and Amy – complained to Margaret about the Board, specifically Luke, being too pushy. Moreover, everyone was forced to keep their water bottles on the table at the far corner at the back of the class.

"Margaret, you should add that 'no chewing gum' rule onto the rules chart," suggested Thomas. "Yeah. After all, you are the one who suggested it in the first place, and you are the President of the Board as well. Hence, you have a say in the administration of the class," added Oliver.

Therefore, Margaret waited for everyone to leave the class for breakfast. Thereafter, she added the rule at the bottom of the chart using a marker. Meanwhile, Amber wrote on the suggestions chart with a dark pen: 'Disband the Board'. The cronies then chuckled out of the classroom slyly.

After breakfast was Magnolia's history lesson. However, before Mr Bill entered the classroom, Amy (the official gum lender of the grade) folded the miscellaneous rule. Finally, when Mr Bill arrived, Luke began bragging about Magnolia's progress as he did with Ms Delilah. Taking that as an opportunity, Margaret said, "Sir, we truly *have* improved in all aspects but one." Saying this, she got up, walked towards the rules chart (pinned onto one of the softboards) and unfolded the 'No chewing gum' rule. "Ah, now this is not correct," began Mr Bill. Thereafter, he gave his classic motivational speech about how Magnolia has the potential to win the award. He also promised the Magnolians chocolates if they won the Best Class Award, claiming that the class obtaining the final Best Class Award of the academic year is technically the best class of the year.

Through the day, the children lavished about their accomplishments to Ms Hendricks, Ms Lancy (who was truly proud of them), Ms Anne, and Ms Fernandes.

Later in the day, the Magnolians had their computer science lesson. During the class, Ms Esther taught the students how to morph photos by deleting their background and pasting them onto another. Therefore, when Ms Esther told the children to explore this tool, a group of Magnolians – namely Hannah, Alice and Luke – searched up an image of Margaret on Google. Upon finding one and asking Margaret's permission to use it, they pasted her face onto the image of deep space. Next, they placed the entire image (Margaret's face in space) inside a lightbulb. When they showed it to the rest of the class, they burst into a thousand laughs.

Their next lesson was physics. The moment Mr Richard entered the class, Alice cried, "Sir, did you know that we put Margaret in space inside a lightbulb?" At this, Mr Richard was confused. However, he took more notice of the cleanliness and behaviour of the class than the statement that Alice just uttered. "What happened to this class? Along with Margaret, did you guys throw the trash also away into space?" At this, the class unanimously narrated their story yet again. Once they were done, Mr Richard made a face of sarcasm as if to say, "Really?"

Likewise, the children continued to work hard and, at the same time, narrate their fascinating story to all the teachers, leaving them dumbstruck.

Finally, one day, the Board and the class unanimously decided to cut off Margaret's rule from the chart. When Margaret returned from lunch, she noticed it was already chopped off.

CHAPTER THIRTY

"Did We Win Best Class?"

A few Tuesdays later, the children were returning from their P.E. class. The whole of Middle School had P.E. block periods every Tuesday and Wednesday, from 10:35 a.m. to 12:05 p.m. During this time, the sun would be blazing and the temperature would be so high that the children's faces would resemble the colour of the expanded alcohol in a thermometer.

The children trod up the stairs and to their respective classrooms, gasping for breath and craving for a gale. It was then that Ms Elizabeth called Margaret. She told her, "Margaret, please tell your class to stay back in class and not go for your next class yet. I need to speak with all of you." Therefore, adhering to Ms Elizabeth's words, Margaret announced that everyone must stay in class and not head to the next one.

In a few minutes, Ms Elizabeth and Ms Lancy were welcomed by the children, who were shockingly sitting in their respective places without creating a commotion. After pausing for a moment to take in the reality, Ms Elizabeth strode towards the front of the class, followed by Ms Lancy, and sat down on the teacher's chair; Ms Lancy took her place behind Ms Elizabeth. Ms Elizabeth looked across the class, into the eyes of each individual student. She looked at their anxious faces. She looked down at a sheet of paper she had in her hands. She placed it on the table, face down. She smiled.

She looked up at the children again and said, "Throughout the year, we teachers have been complaining to you and scolding you about your behaviour. In hindsight, I don't see that's wrong, given the magnitude of your misbehaviour. However, after that rough talk I gave you a few weeks ago, things have begun to change. I have not heard any complaint against you in the last few weeks; the teachers have told me that you are much kinder to them now with minimal to no back answering or rude comments at all; your class looks much neater now. All these things combined, not to mention so many other changes in you, made us teachers think that maybe you deserve a bit more than your current reputation." At this, the children looked at one another in confusion with a green desire in their eyes. Seeing their expressions, Ms Elizabeth and Ms Lancy smiled at one another. Then, Jake suddenly asked, "Ms Elizabeth, did we win Best Class?" Ms Elizabeth gave a sly smile to Jake. She then turned towards the rest of the class and said, "Bull's eye. You indeed *did* win the Best Class Award!" The class remained silent for a moment. Suddenly, once the children had processed what their coordinator had just told them, they exclaimed in unison, "WE WON BEST CLASS!!"

There was an uprise in the class. Everyone was out of their place, jumping triumphantly and jubilantly hugging one another. Then, as if there was some sort of telepathy between the Magnolian minds, they all turned to Margaret.

"Congrats, Margaret!" cried Luke. "None of this would have ever happened but for your unfailing support, encouragement and optimistic approach!" cried Alice. "Oh, no. None of this would have happened if we all weren't in it together. This is an achievement of the entire class – not just a few individuals. All of us contributed in our own ways to make this happen. I too made a little contribution," said Margaret.

After permitting the children to celebrate their victory for a few minutes, Ms Elizabeth requested everyone to return to their seats. Once everyone was calm, Ms Elizabeth handed over the Best Class Award certificate to Ms Lancy who handed it over to Jake and Margaret. Upon receiving the certificate, some other Magnolians rushed to get thumbtacks. Thereafter, Jake and Margaret pinned up the certificate onto their class board, right under the 'MAGNOLIA' written in a big, blue, bold font.

"Smile for the picture!" cried Ms Lancy. The class huddled together in front of the soft board, posing jubilantly as Ms Lancy clicked their picture.

"Three cheers for our class reps, Board of Operations and the whole of Magnolia!" cried Ms Lancy. "Hip-hip, hurray! Hip-hip, hurray! Hip-hip, hurray!" cried the class in unison, laughing in excitement. To them, the news was truly unfathomable. Were they truly the same Magnolians who back answered teachers every class? Were they truly the same Magnolians who could not spend a day without bullying their peers? Were they truly the same Magnolians who misbehaved round the clock? Surprisingly, they sure were!

"What class do you children have next?" asked Ms Elizabeth. "We have library, Ms Elizabeth," replied Margaret, struggling to get her voice across to Ms Elizabeth amidst the tremendous commotion in the class. "Alright, children! You can proceed towards your next class!" Saying this, Ms Elizabeth, followed by Ms Lancy, strode out the classroom door.

The moment they left, the children burst into another uproar of screams, cries and laughter. "Guys, we are already late for class! We should really get going!" cried Margaret. Hence, the children scuttled out of the classroom with a novel in each of their hands. Margaret and Amber left last, switching off the lights and fans. The library was halfway down the corridor and on a bridge that was another connection between the Middle School section and the Elementary section, not to mention the path straight down the corridor. Enroute to the library, the children stopped at Ms Elizabeth's office, from where they would have to leave the main school building and take the bridge to the library. They stared at the softboard that stood on the wall opposite her office. At the sight of another copy of their Best Class Award hanging on the softboard, everyone jumped triumphantly, laughing to their hearts' content. "Please quiet down, children, and head to the library," called Ms Elizabeth from her office.

CHAPTER THIRTY-ONE

ALL'S WELL THAT ENDS WELL...

"Where are you going, Eleanor?" asked Margaret when she saw Eleanor and Laura wandering away into the corridors. "We're bunking library period," replied Eleanor, indifferently. At seeing Margaret's seemingly annoyed expression, she clarified, "We have anyway won best class. Now nobody can force me to behave." "You know, Eleanor, behaving ourselves and staying disciplined isn't just for winning the Best Class Award or pleasing our teachers; it is to build ourselves a good personality so that we grow to become great global citizens," explained Margaret patiently. "You can keep your preachings for the utopian world." Saying this, Eleanor tugged at Laura's arm, and they walked away gossiping about TV shows. Nodding her head side-to-side in disappointment, Margaret responded to Amber's call from the library.

Sitting in the library, barely anyone could keep their eyes on the pages of their books. They were excitedly chattering, trying to fathom and process the occurrence. As they children headed for lunch following library, they spotted Mr Bill and Mr Richard going downstairs for lunch as well. They went rushing towards them to tell them the good news. "Did you hear, sir? We won the Best Class Award!" exclaimed Alice. "Will you give us our chocolates now?" asked Hannah, bells ringing in her voice. "Of course, I will. You guys earned it with your own hard work. Besides, the fact that you won the final Best Class Award of the year implies that you are the best class of the year! Margaret, my dear, can you please send me a reminder email about the chocolates this evening?" asked Mr Bill, kindly. "Sure, sir," replied Margaret. As the Magnolians continued to lavish about their victory to Mr Bill, Mr Richard gave Margaret an eye roll and a facial expression, as if to say, "Is your class for real? You guys are acting like Elementary Schoolers." Margaret giggled.

The next week, the children had their final exams. It was a stressful two weeks for the children, some rote learning their notes while others revising them. However, the weeks passed relatively fast, leading to the children's most dreadful event: the release of their results. However, to most of the children's amusement, they did rather well in their tests! Almost everyone scored more than an 'A' across subjects.

Although the exams had concluded and it had been over two weeks since Magnolia won the Best Class Award, Margaret still had not reminded Mr Bill about the chocolates despite the continuous reminders her peers gave her almost every day. "Margaret!" cried Lewis. "Are you *ever* going to mail him about the chocolates?" "Yeah! I want chocolates!" cried Thomas in agreement. Following Thomas, everyone cried in unison, "WE WANT CHOCOLATES TOO!" "I know you want chocolates, but I just don't know *what* to say to him. How can I ask a teacher to bring us chocolates? Would it not sound rude?"

said Margaret innocently. "Oh, yes, it would be rude if you were doing it out of your own will. However, Mr Bill has *asked* you to remind him about the chocolates," explained Amber. "Besides, tomorrow is the last day of school. And, as far as I remember, we all have continued to remind you to tell him about the chocolates every day since he told you to do so," argued Lewis. "Alright, alright. I shall mail him today for sure," replied Margaret. "She finally got compelled by peer pressure," joked Hannah. "Oh, not peer pressure! Do you all remember that disastrous assembly?" said Amber cynically. "Oh, my bleeding ears! Please don't remind me of that! I want to end seventh grade with good memories," joked Jake.

Finally, the last day of school arrived. Unlike other years, the children were not permitted to wear civil clothes on the last day as the Awards Ceremony was scheduled for the same day, Friday. The awards acknowledged those who scored the highest in each of the subjects, the individual who excelled in academics, the individuals who persevered, and the individual regarded as an all-rounder. The Magnolians were indeed the recipients of majority of the awards, a testimony of their skills and talents.

Following the Awards Ceremony, approximately 2 hours were dedicated for class parties. Each class, along with their homeroom teacher(s), celebrated the completion of yet another year in their own fashion. Although Magnolia was not decorated as much as the other classes, they had the best time! The children smuggled plates after plates of French fries and chicken lollipops from the Elementary School cafeteria, and Ms Lancy had got Margaret and Amber to pop five packets of popcorn kernels for her using the microwave in the teachers' cafeteria, thus adding to the party mood. They played music and danced to their hearts' content. The children even challenged Ms Lancy to play a game with another teacher, wherein the loser had to empty a bottle of water over the other. Sadly, for her, Ms Lancy was compelled to shower an entire bottle of cold water over herself at her losing of the game.

While all the classes in the school had their end-of-year parties, Margaret went around giving her handmade cards with heartfelt messages to all the teachers. Upon returning to Magnolia, she was greeted by a mob of children who were eagerly waiting for Margaret's return so that they could watch a video that they had scripted, directed and video graphed for the graduating batch of Middle School. The video was hilarious wherein the children imitated a day in the life of the graduating grade. The video included scenes of dancing, jamming, playing sports and studying. Just as the children had a good laugh watching their hilarious-yet-realistic video, Mr Richard graciously volunteered to click a photograph of all the Magnolians together.

Right before the children dispersed for lunch, Mr Bill entered the classroom with a large bag in his hand. "Are those our chocolates, sir?" asked Hannah eagerly. "No, they aren't chocolates," he replied. The children's faces shrunk. "As I said before, you are technically the best class of the year since you guys won the last Best Class Award of the year. Therefore, I bought you guys special, Thai, wholewheat, sugar-coated cookies. They are both healthy and delicious at the same time!" The children joyfully accepted the cookies and relished every crumb of it.

The children spent the rest of their days practicing for their annual performing arts event, which was scheduled for the coming Monday. As practice was in the afternoon, when the sun was scorching right overhead, the children truly struggled to stay outdoors. Most of the practices, however, went on smoothly. The Elementary School dances and the Middle School dances went on without any hiccups. However, there was one dance that a grade of High School, and Margaret, performed. Since this was a classical dance, the students were compelled to take off their shoes. However, given the extreme heat, the children ran off stage sequentially, as and when their endurance wore off. Margaret's friends, seeing that she was in pain due to her feet burning on the stage, took off her socks and poured a bottle of cold water on her feet. The High Schoolers too took the idea and got riddance from their pain. However, their feet felt numb throughout the day.

Considering that it was the last day of school, the teachers permitted the children to collect their phones earlier than usual. Thus, all the children were clicking away, capturing memories of their class, friends and school on their phones.

On Monday, the entire school was radiating all the hype and pomp that the students felt. The parents arrived an hour after the students did and were taken around for viewing the art gallery that was made especially for this day, collating the artwork of all the students throughout the academic year. In addition, there were food stalls at the entrance of the school that served scrumptious sweets and savouries, not to mention beverages like tea, coffee and freshly squeezed lemonade. The P.E. field was the venue of the main events. The stage was black and ginormous, as big as the entire basketball court. Moreover, the sound system was stellar and the stage had a 4K-quality LED screen. The adjacent football court was used for seating all the parents under a large shamiana. As the parents trickled in, the children were upstairs in the main school building, doing their makeup and hair for one another. Finally, when it was showtime, everyone hurried downstairs.

The fest started off with a blast. The opening act, which was a choir performance of the song 'This is the Greatest Show' accompanied live by an in-house band and the dance students exhibiting their grace & energy, truly set the mood for the fest. Following the opening act were choir performances. The school choir, comprising of over a hundred students across grades, sang a set of songs that were the perfect blend of power and melody. Next up were the Elementary School dances. These were arranged in a theme: the elements of nature. Thus, there were groups of children that represented the forest biome, the desert biome, the arctic biome and the like. This was when things began going downhill.

Unfortunately, it began raining. Therefore, everyone was rushed into the main school building, and all the equipment were covered with sheets of tarpaulin. Everyone waited for the rains to stop. Half an hour passed. One hour passed. One and a half hours. Two hours. The rains pelted unceasingly. Therefore, the activities department decided to shift all the remaining acts to the multiple audiovisual (AV) rooms that the school had. However, Ms Arora (one of the dance teachers) announced that the Middle & High School dances were cancelled due to lack of space. "We cannot manage fifty teenagers inside one AV room along with an audience," she justified.

"Well, I guess the fest was unfortunately a washout," said Amy finally. "Well, at least we had a good year. I don't know about you, but I'm eagerly awaiting the next school year!" exclaimed Margaret, as they walked out the school gates.

From The Same Author

Now available on Amazon, Flipkart and Kindle

The author can be reached at :
sivaraj.ananthakrishnan@gmail.com

About The Author

Akshara Sivaraj is a Grade 8 student. She is an avid reader, science enthusiast and likes to travel and explore the world and beyond.

In addition to writing, she also has a passion for classical music and dance.

Her prior 3 publications - titled 'Hampi : The Timeless Treasure', 'Plan(ET) B : Our Second Chance' and 'Ellora & Ajanta : Mysteries Unshrouded' - are available in various platforms such as Amazon, Flipkart and Kindle and are globally well received.

Through her writings, Akshara wishes to bring about the change that she wishes to see in the world, resulting in the betterment of humanity at large.

AKSHARA SIVARAJ